Archdruid

Rogues of Magic Book 2

Tiffany Shand

DEDICATION

For my mum, Karen.

CHAPTER 1

Urien ran his fingers along his father's seat of power. The throne itself was made from dark dryad oak. Almost like a tree, it twisted in three different directions to form the back of the seat. Two much higher branches rose in the front of the throne. Carved on the front of the backrest was a white oak tree surrounded by three stars—Darius' own personal emblem. The ancient throne had seated more than one archdruid over the last few thousand years. It hummed and vibrated with power. Ann had always said she'd seen glowing lines of energy flowing through it. Urien saw no such thing.

He made a move to sit down, but hesitated. Why couldn't he bring himself to sit here? It was just a stupid chair after all. It meant nothing. Still, it felt good being back in the physical world again. He'd been trapped on the other side for so long part of him feared he'd wake up back there only to find it had all been a dream.

This was no dream. Urien was here, back in his rightful place as leader of Caselhelm. Soon the other lands would be under his control. One way or another, they would all fall in line.

The first thing he'd done was lock his mother up in the dungeon. She may have been loyal and helped overthrow Darius and his followers, but Urien had been born to rule. He would not share his power with anyone. He was annoyed she hadn't died yet. The bitch had proved stronger than he'd thought.

You're afraid of sitting where he sat, aren't you? Xander asked.

Urien winced at the sound of his brother's voice. Why couldn't Xander just shut up and go away? He picked up a small mirror someone had left lying near the throne. But it wasn't his true face that stared back at him. Xander had short, dark brown hair, pale skin, and a handsome face. He also had their father's pale blue eyes. How Urien hated those eyes! He'd have much preferred to see his own dark brown, almost black ones staring back at him. His own face, with his mop of curly black hair. Yet here he was, stuck inside the body of his younger half-brother.

Be quiet, or I'll do away with you. I want you to die almost as much as I want my wretched mother gone from this world, Urien said. He tried his best to ignore Xander's voice and not talk to him. At times, it proved impossible.

Guess I shouldn't be surprised you'd kill your own mother after what you did to our father and my mother, Xander remarked. *You haven't changed. I doubt*

6

you even have remorse for everything you've done.

Oh, do be quiet, brother. Your thoughts are so irritating. Besides, my mother isn't dead. Yet. Urien cast the mirror aside and sat down on the throne, just to prove to Xander he wasn't afraid. Nothing happened. *See, I'm not afraid. This is my throne now. My seat. My land.*

This seat glowed and vibrated with power whenever Darius had sat upon it. Yet Urien felt nothing. Not even a stirring or crackle of energy.

You're in my body. Get used to it, Xander snapped. *I won't let you reject my spirit. I'll fight you every step of the way. I'll be the conscience you've never had.*

Conscience, ha. A conscience serves no purpose. Urien laughed out loud as Constance, his new lead Gliss, came into the room.

"Connie, my love, tell me: is Ceara broken yet?"

Connie, with her blond braid and olive skin, looked dark compared to his old favourite Ceara's porcelain complexion. She wore a black leather bodysuit that covered her from neck to toe.

"She's strong, my lord. Our usual methods aren't working." Connie paused. "I have good news. We have control of Trin. Our forces broke through the island's protections."

"Good." His first task in getting the other races to start falling in line would be to prove to them he, not Ann, had the power and rank of the archdruid.

You didn't deserve Ceara. Even as a Gliss, she was too good for you. Xander's voice continued to taunt him.

"Quiet," Urien hissed, gripping the sides of the throne so hard the wood shuddered.

"My lord?" Constance frowned.

Urien stormed out of the hall and down to the dungeon. Ceara hung from the ceiling. Every inch of her body black and purple. Her long black hair fell like a curtain over her pale skin, greasy and matted in places. Dried blood covered her lips and ears from where the shock rods had been placed on her.

"I do so hate seeing you like this." Urien motioned for the Gliss to lower Ceara.

The chains clanked as Ceara came down. Her dark eyes opened as he ran a finger down her chin. Strange; she still looked oddly beautiful, even in this horrific state.

"Your beauty doesn't deserve to be marred like this." He smiled. "If you swear loyalty to me again, you won't have to go through any more of this."

"You replaced me, you bastard," Ceara spat. "I did everything for you, stayed loyal to you all these years. Now you're with her." Her eyes flashed as she turned her gaze to Connie, who stood behind him.

Urien saw fire in her eyes even after days of endless torture. She'd proven stronger than he'd thought. That fire, that strength, made him fall in love with her in the first place. Had it been real love? He thought it had been, once. Only the gods knew if he was truly capable of such a thing. Nothing mattered to him more than power. That was the only good trait he'd inherited from his bastard father.

"You betrayed me. I know you've been working with and helping the resistance over the years. It's all here in Xander's mind." He tapped his forehead. "You helped my sister escape. You had to be punished, don't you see that?"

Ceara looked away. "She's stronger than you, and the real archdruid. She'll stop you."

"Ah, yes, but she can't kill me, thanks to our bastard father. I'm more powerful than ever, now I have Xander's power." He caressed her cheek. "You can come back. Be my favourite again. Wouldn't you like that?"

"Nothing you say will ever make me come back to you." She spat at him.

A bloody trickle of saliva hit his face. He wiped it off with the back of his hand. "I know you, Ceara. Deep down inside that twisted heart of yours, you're just like me. That's why you chose me instead of my brother." Urien drew back and grinned at her. "Part of you still longs for my brother, doesn't it? You could have both of us now." He ran a finger over her chafed lips. "Come back to me. Be mine again."

Her dark eyes flashed. "You're more twisted than I thought to think I'd ever want you. You might be in Xander's body, but he's twice the man you'll ever be. Face it. You're nothing. You'll never be half of what your father was, either." Her lips twisted into a smile.

Urien's jaw clenched and he glared at Constance. "You've been too soft on her." He grabbed one of the shock rods and pressed it to Ceara's chest. Electricity jolted through her, streams of blue static radiating across her body. He knew the pain had to be excruciating.

Ceara gritted her teeth, tears streaming down her face.

Stop! Xander cried. The thought he was causing Xander pain only brought Urien more pleasure.

He pressed the rod to her heart. Her body trembled, convulsing. She slumped forward, dead. "Bring her back."

Constance yanked Ceara's body down on to the floor, the chains clanking as she did so. She opened Ceara's mouth and breathed air back into her lungs, performing chest compressions until Ceara's heart started beating again.

Ceara coughed and glared at them. "Kill me as many times as you want, Urien. I'll never come back to you," she hissed. "Ann will stop you. When I get free, I'll damn well help her destroy you."

Urien stormed out, fists clenched.

See, she's strong, Xander goaded. *Not everyone will fall in line, brother, no matter how hard you try to break them. You're a failure.*

"No!" Urien screamed, hitting the wall so hard the stone exploded with a burst of energy. Shards of rock shot in all directions. Pain exploded across his knuckles and his hand came away bloody.

"My lord?" Constance said. "What's wrong? You've hurt yourself."

"I want her broken and on our side. I can't trust the others to keep control of Trin." He grabbed Constance by the throat. "You must go. Take Ceara with you, I want her out of my sight. If you can't break her, kill her. I won't have any of my Gliss turning against me."

"Yes, my lord." Constance bowed her head. "We'll leave at once."

His hand throbbed, but he ignored the pain and blood.

You'll never control Trin…

Urien shut Xander's voice out and stomped up the steps toward the tower where his mother now lived. He nodded to the two Gliss standing guard. The Gliss had sworn loyalty to him, not his mother. At least they had the sense know he had the true power. Orla had only been keeping the throne warm for him during his imprisonments in the nether realm. He'd never intended her to rule, but she hadn't been keen on handing all her power over to him.

The spelled lock on the door flared with runes as he pressed his palm against it, unlocking it. He pushed open the cell door. The room appeared tiny, with little more than a metal bunk and a bucket in the corner for her to relieve herself in. Small slivers of pale light came through the thin barred window. It cast faint white pools across the grimy flagstone floor.

Urien's breath came out as mist as he stepped into the freezing room. The window offered no protection from the elements outside. It let in both the rain and the wind. Dampness covered the grey stone walls. Too bad the elements had little effect on his demon mother.

Orla sat staring out of the barred window. Her long black tresses fell past her shoulders. Her pale skin shone almost like moonlight. Her black eyes narrowed on him as he stood in the doorway of her cell. Sometimes he hated how alike they looked.

"Why did you bring me back in this damned body?" Urien demanded. "Why didn't you cast his spirit out? His voice is driving me mad!" After a month of hearing Xander's taunts, cries, and accusations, he didn't know how much more he could take. There had to be a way to rip his brother's damned soul from this body.

"I saved you from the hell your sister cast you into." Orla turned around to face him.

Urien's hand shook as Xander tried to regain control of his body. "Look at me, Mother. I can't look weak. The other leaders won't even answer my summons. They don't believe I'm the archdruid." He fell to his knees and buried his face in her lap. "Help me." For a moment, he wanted her to hold him as any mother would hold their child to comfort them.

Orla had never been that kind of mother.

She shoved him away in disgust. "What's the matter with you?" she spat. "I kept hold of Caselhelm for all these years. You were born to lead the five lands, and yet here you are, cowering like a wounded puppy. I overthrew the Valeran rule so you could take your place as Darius' heir!"

Urien clutched his head, grabbing handfuls of his hair. "Xander's voice torments me night and day."

"Ignore him. This is your body now. You're more powerful than ever before. Start acting like it, boy." She placed her hands on his shoulders.

Urien's fists clenched. "How am I more powerful? You have an army of two thousand. You control the city, but what about the rest of these lands?" Urien pulled away from her and rose to his feet. "A few thousand men and a couple dozen Gliss do not make me a leader. I want all the lands. I want to watch the other races cower before me, yet here I am, walled up in the palace with you."

"Then you must prove to them you—not your sister—are the true leader. A true leader doesn't wait for power; they take it. You can't allow Rhiannon to start rallying people to her side." Orla's stood and took hold of his hands. "You have everything you need to stop her. Stop whining and act like a true ruler. Be the archdruid and the people will bow before you."

"I have Trin, and soon the rest will follow. I'll wipe those damn druids off the face of Erthea. How did Darius get them all in line?" He pushed his hair—no, Xander's hair—off his face. Everything about this body felt strange and alien to him, like wearing clothes that were too tight.

"He used the forbidden arts. He used magic that went far beyond any druid power."

"Father must have kept his knowledge somewhere. He taught Rhiannon things he never showed me." Urien rubbed his chin. "I need his knowledge. It would give me an advantage over Rhiannon."

"Think, my son. Darius couldn't keep everything locked inside his mind. He must have kept his secret somewhere. He used to disappear at times and then he'd reappear again."

Urien's brow creased as he searched through his memories, then Xander's.

"I followed Father one night out into the grounds. I saw him open a door before he vanished. That must be it." His smile faded. "I still need a way to get the other races to fall in line."

"Do what you do best. Either they join you or you kill them all."

13

Orla smirked.

CHAPTER 2

Ann Valeran stared at the tranquil waters surrounding the small island of Trin, the druids' sacred island. It stood alone and forlorn without the heavy mists that usually protected it. Its rolling green hills looked darker, not glowing with their usual brightness. Even the grey stone tower that sat atop the tor looked foreboding now. "Someone has broken down the wards," she remarked. Her long blond hair fluttered around her face as she pulled back the hood of her long black leather cloak.

"There are Gliss over there, no doubt." Sage scowled and brushed dirt off the hem of her long blue robe. "This place has belonged to our people for the last three thousand years without ever falling into enemy hands. We need to get them off the island."

"But how did they do it? Like you said, the island's protections have kept it safe. Urien must have found a way through." She clenched her fists at the thought of her elder half-brother. Anger would do her little good. "We'll get it back." Ann raised her hand and muttered words of power to summon a boat made of reeds that would carry them to the island. *"Bád le feiceáil."*

Edward and Jax came up behind her. Ed, with his long brown hair and golden-brown eyes, looked the opposite of his foster brother, Jax. Jax had dark skin, a bald head, and a chiselled face. Ed wore his usual black ranger clothes, whilst Jax wore the old black cloak and trousers left over from his days in the Black Guard.

Ed had been her best friend for most of her life, and partner for almost a decade. It still felt odd having Jax back in their lives. Still, it was good to have their old friend back.

"Do you sense Urien nearby?" Ed asked her.

Ann shook her head. "No, I don't sense anyone on the island, just a few guards. No doubt there will be Gliss there."

"We'll be ready," Jax said, drawing his staff.

Ann frowned and glanced at the empty shoreline. No boat had appeared. "They must have broken all of the island's enchantments." She gritted her teeth. How could Urien and a few Gliss have wiped out the magic that had existed on the island for so long? It had only been a few weeks since her last encounter with her brother. Since then, Ann and the others had tried to stay one step ahead of him.

"Perhaps we don't need to go there," Sage said, running her fingers through her long red hair that was streaked with grey. "The island is connected to the power of the archdruid." The druid pushed her hair off her face as the wind off the eastern sea picked up. Her green eyes and weathered skin seemed dull compared to when Ann had first seen her again a few weeks earlier.

Ann flinched at the word "archdruid." She still hadn't come to terms with that role. Despite her father dying five years earlier, she'd never thought of herself as the archdruid—the leader of all the druids. She'd been in hiding since her father, the former archdruid and leader of Caselhelm, had been murdered by Urien, along with her mother. Darius had been the strongest and most powerful leader among the races. He'd controlled three out of the five lands—something no one had ever done. His death had plunged the lands into another war when Urien and his mother, Orla, had brought about the revolution.

Ann had ripped Urien's soul from his body when she discovered her parents dead and sent it into another land. She'd spent all these years trying to stop Orla from ever bringing him back, but she'd failed. Now Urien's soul resided in the body of her other brother, Xander. Urien's own body remained locked away and hidden where he'd never find it.

Urien was back and more determined than ever to take their father's place and take leadership among the five lands.

Ann knew she had to find a way to get Urien's spirit out and save Xander. First, they had to stop Urien from getting the power of Trin. Having the druids' isle would give him an unwanted advantage over them.

"That connection is no good now there are Gliss over there." Ann sighed. "It won't be enough for me to do much." Whatever connection she may have had to the island would be severed.

Gliss were women with empathic abilities trained in the arts of pain and torture. They used their gifts to inflict pain and suffering on their victims. Gliss could kill with a single touch by reflecting someone's emotions back at them. Ann hated the thought of them being on the Druid's sacred island, defiling it with their dark magic. She only hoped they hadn't taken anyone prisoner there. But she doubted anyone would have been left there. After Flora's death, Sage hadn't been back, and there had been no one else to become the island's guardians.

"The island is a source of natural energy, the very energy druids use. It's part of our connection to Erthea," Sage said. "No Gliss can break such a deep connection. You must sink the island. The sea will keep Trin and its power safe from Urien."

"What about the people already on the island?" Jax asked, digging the end of his double-edged staff into the ground. "Will they be protected, too?"

"No, they'll be dragged into the water," Sage answered. "Good riddance. May the spirits have mercy on them when they reach Summerland."

Ann's eyes widened. She'd never thought of her father's old adviser as bloodthirsty. Maybe losing Flora had changed Sage.

"If they try to make it ashore, we'll take care of them," Ed said.

"Jax and I will stay here. Ann, you should go around the other side of the shore. The closer you are to the island, the better." Sage motioned for her to go.

Ann reluctantly nodded. She still didn't like the idea of submerging the island, but what other choice did they have? Even if they fought and regained control over it, Urien would only keep sending more people to steal it back. Over the past few years on the run, she'd never been able to afford the luxury of staying in one place for too long. Maybe one day that would change.

Ann trudged along the shoreline, keeping a shield around herself as her long black leather cloak billowed behind her. The grass felt squishy underneath her boots. She breathed in the familiar scent of salt and grass with a deep breath. Her heart tightened.

You have to do this, she told herself. *There's no other way. You'll see the island again someday. It won't be gone forever.* Ann knew her shield wouldn't do much good. Any Gliss would be able to see her if they looked out across the shoreline. But it made her feel a little safer.

Ed trailed behind her.

"I can't believe I'm even considering this," she muttered. "Trin was a second home to us. How can I sink it to the bottom of the sea?"

"We don't have another choice. It's either that or Urien will find a way to harness its power." Ed glanced round the shoreline.

"I can't stay here, either. We would be stuck constantly fending off Urien's attacks," Ann said.

"At least it'll be safe down there."

Yes, but she hated the idea of not coming here. This place had been her only refuge over the past few tumultuous years. A safe haven whenever she or the others accused of using magic in Caselhelm needed to escape from Orla. She had no idea where she would take refugees and people who were hunted now. Trin had always been the first place they came to before her contacts in the resistance helped them move on to new places and start new lives.

"What happens after this?" Ed asked. "We've been fighting off Urien's men and Gliss over the past few weeks while our way here. What comes after?"

Ann scowled. "We take Sage to Trewa. It's the last surviving druid settlement. She should be—" She almost said "safe," but where was anyone safe within the five lands anymore? "She wants to go there," she said instead. "My only goal is to find a way to stop Urien and save Xander. If the druids can help, then that's where we'll go." She glanced back at him. "What about you?"

Ed frowned. "What about me?" He ran a hand through his long hair, something he always did when anxious.

"You've been struggling to keep control of your beast. Are you…?" Ann couldn't bring herself to ask him if he'd leave. Like Trin, he'd been the one constant in her life. She didn't know what she'd do if he left.

"I'm fine," Edward insisted.

Ann knew better, but said nothing else. She stopped at the edge of the bank. The island loomed in front of her, with its sloping green hills and the tower that stood proudly on top of the tor. A lump rose in her throat as she stared at it. Ann took a deep breath, raised her hands, and said the words of power. *"Doirtealáil Trin bhun na farraige."* The old druid tongue flowed off her lips easily. Light flared between her fingers and enveloped the island, radiating blue energy.

Nothing happened.

Ann frowned and said the words again. *"Doirtealáil Trin bhun na farraige."*

Still nothing.

"What's wrong?" Ed asked.

Ann shook her head. "I don't know, it's not working. Maybe Urien did something." A cool breeze blew in off the sea, ruffling her hair and filling the air with the scents of salt and seaweed.

"Sage seems to think nothing can break the connection you have to the island."

Sage isn't right about everything.

"Maybe your resistance is blocking your connection," Ed suggested.

Her blue eyes flashed. "What resistance?"

"Trying to deny you're the archdruid."

"I have the power, but I'm not the archdruid." Heck, she'd had to keep her magic usage to a minimum during her years on the run. Some of her former skills had grown rusty over time. She'd get the hang of it again.

Ed put a hand on her shoulder. "You are, Ann. You need to accept that if you want to defeat Urien."

"Just like you accept your beast now?" She arched a brow.

He looked away. "That's different. I was turned into a beast. You

21

were born for this. Darius taught and trained you as his heir because he knew you were the strongest out of his children," Ed said. "You can do this."

"Some archdruid I am. I couldn't even save Xander." Her heart ached just thinking of her younger brother. Ann didn't know if Urien had forced Xander's spirit out, or if he remained trapped inside his own body. She hadn't had a chance to check on Xander once Urien's spirit had taken over.

"You're not infallible." Ed wrapped an arm around her shoulders. "I know you'll figure out a way to get him back."

She leaned into him and squeezed his hand. He'd been there for her through everything. The three months he'd been Orla's prisoner had been the worst of her life. But he was back, and she wouldn't lose him again.

Ann closed her eyes and sent her senses out. The island hummed with energy, glowing like a beacon to her druid sight. Pools of rainbow-coloured light danced around the island. Its protection might be gone, but its magic remained. She felt the connection there, like an invisible cord tethered to her. Her eyes blurred with power that rose from deep inside her. Ann hadn't felt so much power for so long after years of keeping it locked away. It felt good to let it out again.

She repeated the words of power, opened her eyes, and light enveloped the island. The presence of people flickered at the edge of her mind. The earth groaned as it slowly began to submerge beneath the waves.

"It's working." Ed grinned.

The deep blue waves of the eastern ocean swallowed the grass. It washed over the tiny beach with its golden yellow sand, swept up the pathways and through the apple orchard. It sucked everything under until only the tor itself hovered like a tiny island on the water.

Then the great tower vanished into the depths, disappearing from view.

She let her arms fall to her side and sank to her knees, her energy spent as she took several deep breaths.

"You alright?" Ed knelt beside her and touched her shoulder.

"There are people escaping. Go take care of them," Ann breathed, motioning to the figures moving in the distance. "I'll be fine."

Ed hesitated then took off, blurring in the opposite direction.

"That was incredible." Sage smiled as she walked over to Ann's side. "I haven't seen so much power in decades. I'm not sure even your father could have pulled it off."

Ann's eyes narrowed. "You never mentioned that. What if it hadn't worked?"

The old druid chuckled, and her lips twisted into a smile. "I knew it would work. You are much more powerful than you give yourself credit for."

Ann pushed her long wavy blond hair off her face, still breathing hard. "I'm exhausted." She'd noticed the dark circles under her eyes earlier, and knew they'd be deeper now. Probably even visible when she reapplied her glamour spell to disguise her true appearance. She slumped back against the grass. Beneath her fingers pulsed the Erthea lines—lines of natural energy that were the lifeblood of the world of Erthea. She raised her hand, causing veins of cracking green energy to splinter across the ground as she drew power from them. The light shot up, bathing her body in a green hue. It felt like cool water washing over her as she drew the energy in and felt it restore some of her strength.

"That's because you channelled too much energy," Sage said. "Take more of what you need from the earth."

I don't need to be told that. Ann suspected she needed the island's supply of energy to feel better. She reached down again, drew more power. Light washed over her. Nature gave druids their power, but fire was her own element. That gave her strength like no other element could. Too bad she didn't have time to start a fire now.

"We should reach Trewa in two days," Ann said, brushing grass off her leather trousers as she rose. "Are you sure you want to stay there? You can travel with us—"

Sage shook her head. "I'm too old for travel." Her red hair seemed almost white now. "With Flora gone, I want to live my days among our people."

Ann's heart twisted at the mention of her aunt, Flora, who'd died during Urien's re-emergence. Flora had been Sage's wife. It had only been a month since Flora's death, and the pain still felt raw for all of them. Sage must've felt it just as keenly. Sage and her aunt had been a couple for over thirty years. Ann couldn't imagine the kind of pain she was going through.

"Don't worry about me. You are going to have a long road ahead of you." Sage rose to her feet. "Urien will need allies if he is to become as powerful as your father was."

Ann snorted. "I hear he's already telling everyone he's the archdruid. He's killing anyone who refuses to join him." She knew sooner or later she'd have to face her brother again, but Jax had been gathering intel for her as much as he could.

"That's why you must get to people before he does," Sage said. "Urien can't be everywhere at once. You must convince the other races to join your side."

"And then what?" Ann asked. "I've been in hiding for almost five years whilst Orla laid waste to most of Caselhelm. Even if I get the other races on my side, then what? I'm not my father; I'm just one person. I can't command armies, nor do I want to. Plus, most of the other races aren't very welcoming to the archdruid—someone who used to help enslave many of them. This isn't like the realm wars." She glanced along the shoreline to check for any signs of fleeing Gliss or guards who might have escaped the sinking island. "This fight is between Urien and me, not the other races."

"Urien will drag the other races into this. He wants to have the kind of power and influence your father had. You need them on your side," Sage said. "I know you never wanted to be the archdruid, but you can't walk away from that path any longer."

Ann shook her head. "I'm not the—" She scowled when Sage frowned at her. "I don't want to be the leader of anything. I just want to get Xander back and stop Urien."

"And then what?" Sage asked, hands on her hips. "If you did both those things, what would you do? The five lands are still in chaos. The people who murdered your parents still haven't been brought to justice. You know as well as I do there were more than Urien or Orla involved. Someone very powerful helped them."

Ann shrugged. After being in hiding for so long, she'd never allowed herself to consider that possibility. She knew it would take years, if not her entire life, to stop the people responsible for murdering her family and bring freedom to the five lands.

"I'll find those responsible; I'm getting close. I couldn't find answers before due to Orla's influence. Now Urien is back, I have a greater chance of finding who helped them," she said. "Once I succeed, I'd like to have a real home again. Maybe live among the other druids. I don't want to be the archdruid, or a ruler. That's not who I am."

"Just because you don't call yourself Rhiannon anymore doesn't mean you stopped being a Valeran. Your father was the first archdruid to ever become a leader among the races—the leader of all leaders," Sage said. "He didn't raise you to live in the shadows, either."

Ann winced at the mention of her full name. "I agreed to come with you to Trewa, don't push it," she said. She moved along the shore as a woman dressed in a brown leather bodysuit scrambled onto the bank, her long dark hair plastered to her face. A Gliss.

Ann pulled out her knives that she kept sheathed to her back and flung one at the Gliss before she had a chance to attack. It hit the Gliss in the chest and she slumped to the ground, dead. Her body fell back into the water, a bright pool of red spreading out around her.

"One down. I need to check on Ed."

CHAPTER 3

Ed snarled, fangs bared, as he slashed at the first Gliss who came at him with his claws. His inner beast had taken control the instant he'd sensed danger.

Jax swung his double-edged staff around, slashing two guards as they tried to grab him. He struck both down.

Ed blocked the Gliss's next blow as she came at him with a small metal shock rod equipped with magic that could burn through flesh and bone, causing unimaginable pain. He winced as it grazed his arm, sending a burning pain across his skin and grabbed the Gliss by the throat. She hissed at him and raised her hand. Light flared between her fingers and on her forehead as she unleashed her magic.

Energy rippled against his skin as she used her magic to tap into his emotions and turn his power against him. Her magic vibrated against him like an oncoming storm. It only infuriated his beast even more. Ed's eyes flashed emerald, their light reflected in the Gliss' own eyes. He squeezed hard until they rolled back in her head. He snapped her neck and grabbed the next Gliss. She hit him hard, then kicked him in the stomach.

Ed stumbled backward. *Guess I'm not as strong as I thought.*

She threw one of her knives at him. It embedded itself in his shoulder. Ed grunted as he felt a sting of pain, but it would heal. He yanked it out before she had a chance to activate the magic held within it and threw it at her faster than she could blink. It lodged in her throat and her eyes widened in shock before she slumped to the ground, dead.

Ed felt the beast, the strange, powerful entity that now resided in his body along with him. Rage and bloodlust heated through his veins; he wanted to kill again. To feel the warm blood on his hands, to taste it.

"Hey, I think we got all of them," Ann called as she ran over to them. "I got two Gliss and a guard already."

"Shame, I was starting to have fun," Jax said and lowered his staff.

"There are plenty more where they came from," Ann said, walking over to Ed. "Ed, are you alright?"

His fists clenched as he tried to regain control of his body. *Back,* he thought, trying to force to force the beast back into the cage of his mind. *Back!*

"You're bleeding." Ann touched his shoulder.

Ed threw out his arm to shove her away. "Stay back," he hissed. The force of the movement sent Ann flying through the air. She landed a few feet away.

Ed gasped. Both his fangs and claws retracted. Spirits, had he hurt her? "What the heck are you doing, brother?" Jax demanded, flashing him a glare as he hurried over to Ann. "You alright?"

She nodded as Jax helped her up. "I'm fine."

"Ann, I'm…" Ed tried to form words, but couldn't. The one thing he'd feared happening just had. He'd hurt the one person he cared about most. Deep down, he'd known this might happen sooner or later. Spirits, what if he had done worse than knock her over?

"It's okay, I'm not injured." She pushed her hair off her face and her hand came away bloody.

Ed turned and blurred away. He couldn't believe it. He'd vowed he'd die before he ever hurt her, or anyone else he cared about. Now he had without even meaning to. *I have to leave. I have to get this thing out of me! One way or another, I will get rid of this thing.*

Ed stopped at the edge of the shoreline. Where he could he go? Trin had gone now, and he hadn't had a real home in over five years. Ann and Jax were the only family he had left. As much as it pained him to leave, he knew he couldn't stay for much longer.

But where can I go? Nowhere will be safe for me, even if I wear a glamour. Plus, I could be putting innocent lives at risk.

"Ed." Ann ran over to him. "What's wrong? Why are you—?"

"I'm sorry." He avoided her gaze and flinched when she reached out to touch him. *I can't believe I hurt her.*

"It's—"

Ed felt waves of comfort coming from her through their combined mind link. He didn't want comfort; he wanted to get away. "It's not okay. I could have killed you. I can't even be around you anymore."

"You can't kill me. I can't die, and I know you didn't mean it." She crossed her arms.

"This thing inside me is getting stronger by the day," Ed said, running his hand through his hair. "It's trying to take control of me. I'd never forgive myself if I hurt you."

"You didn't hurt me, and you won't." Ann stared at him. "Are you really going to leave?"

"What other choice do I have?" Ed demanded. He tried to raise a mental shield inside his mind, conjuring the image of a stone wall. He didn't know if it would work. "I need to be rid of this thing."

"We're going to Trewa. My uncle is there. He and the other druids may be able to help," she said. "You can't just leave. Urien will be looking for you, too. If he captures you—"

"You know I'd never betray you, but I can't say you're safe around me."

Ann reached up and cupped his face with her hands. "You can learn to control this, and I promise I'll do everything I can to help," she said, pressing her forehead against his. "Just don't leave. I can't lose anyone else right now."

"I'm a danger to you." He pulled away, missing the feel of her closeness.

Ann shook her head. "You made me a promise—*we* made a promise to always be there for each other. Always and forever, remember?"

Ed smiled at their childhood promise. One of the few things that meant something. The memory calmed him and washed away some of his anguish. He'd been one of the Black Guard, a group of elite soldiers who had once protected and served the archdruid. He'd sworn to serve Darius. That vow now extended to her. He hadn't stayed because of his vow or any promise he made to her. He stayed because she was the most important person in his life.

"I remember, and alright, I won't leave you—not yet." Where would he go? Most of the races were either enslaved under the control of the different leaders or had sworn their loyalty to Orla. He doubted anywhere in the five lands was safe anymore. And who had more power than the archdruid herself?

If anyone could help him, it would be her. Ed took a deep breath, trying to calm the growling beast inside the cage of his mind.

"Good, because I know you can control this." She squeezed his shoulder.

Ed didn't want to control it. He wanted to get rid of it and return to what he had been before. Now he didn't know what he was. Ed couldn't even use magic the way he once had, and he hated it. Being one of the Black and serving Darius had given him a purpose in life. Working with Ann had too. But he didn't have any sense of identity anymore. This beast felt strange, alien, and he hated the way it hungered for blood and death. How long would he be able to contain the beast before it fully took control of him?

"I won't accept this, Ann. I wasn't born this way."

Splashing and the thump of a heartbeat made Ed turn his attention to the embankment. "There's someone else in the water." He moved to the edge of the bank and saw someone struggling to break to the surface. Long black hair hovered just above the surface as someone flayed about. "It's a woman. I can't see if she is a Gliss or not." Ed spotted the figure of another woman in a leather bodysuit running along the other side of the shore.

"Help the woman. I'll get the Gliss." Ann sprinted off in the opposite direction.

Ed wanted to protest, but jumped into the water, surprised he didn't feel any ice given the time of year. He swam toward her. Her head began to disappear, leaving only her hair floating above the surface. He dove under, grabbed her by the waist, and pulled her to the surface, then dragging her to the shore.

"Are you alright?" Ed asked.

The woman's long hair fell over her face as she coughed. Her feet and ankles were shackled with chains. He inhaled to sense if she were a Gliss or not. Her scent remained masked by salt and the stench of seaweed and blood. Ed guessed she must've been a prisoner, and caught hold of the chains, breaking them apart. The beast gave him unnatural strength too. He did the same with the ones on her ankles. "It's alright, you're safe now." Ed caught a trace of her scent: lavender. He'd know that scent anywhere,

The woman pushed her hair off her face and stared up at him

through blackened eyes. "Thanks for the rescue, wolfy." Ceara smirked despite her swollen, crackled lips. She looked almost as he remembered, with pale white skin and dark—almost black—irises. Only a leather strip covered her breasts, and a larger strip covered her thighs.

Ed snarled at the sight of the Gliss. "You!" He couldn't believe he saved a Gliss of all people. It didn't matter she'd once been his foster sister. She still betrayed them by joining Urien. Because of her, he'd been turned into a beast. He made a move to grab her, and Ceara shrank back.

"Not going to kill an unarmed woman, are you, wolfy?" Ceara said, pushing her dripping hair off her face.

"Just because you're unarmed doesn't mean you aren't dangerous. Stop calling me that." He glared at her. "You stopped being my sister a long time ago." Using his childhood nickname wouldn't make him feel any pity toward her. Not after everything she'd done.

Ann hurried over to them and frowned. "Ceara, what are you doing here?"

"I was being held prisoner on the island—before it sank," Ceara said and scrambled up. "I'm guessing that was you?" Ed caught her wincing as she fell back down.

They hadn't seen Ceara since she'd helped in their last attempt to stop Urien a month earlier. Ed had hoped that would be the last time they ever saw her again. Just because she'd helped them didn't make her an ally.

"Let's kill her and be done with it." Ed made a move toward the

Gliss.

Ann caught hold of his arm. "Don't," she said. "She's hurt."

"Ann, the only good Gliss is a dead one," he snapped. "She'll go running back to Urien—"

Ceara snorted. "Do I look like I want to go back to Urien or the Gliss?" she demanded, rising on wobbly legs. "I'd rather die than go back to them. I've been imprisoned ever since we last saw each other."

"We can't let you go either, can we?" Ed retorted. He couldn't believe Ann seemed to be taking pity on her. Since when did they help Gliss? They killed them; they didn't help them. Gliss were the enemy.

Ceara's body had black and purple bruises covering almost every inch of it. Ed knew full well what the Gliss were capable of.

"Let me stay with you," Ceara said to Ann. "I can help you. You know I helped the resistance for years whilst I worked for Orla. Maybe I can help you stop Urien."

Ed snorted. "Yeah, right. You'll betray us, like you did when we went to meet you in that bunker. You kidnapped me and turned me into a beast." He crossed his arms. *Ann, you can't be serious about working with her. She'll use us just like she did last time. We can't afford to trust her again.*

Ann knelt to examine the bruises. "You need healing."

"Magic won't work very well on me. I'm a Gliss."

Jax, get here now, Ed ordered. *Hurry.*

Jax swooped down in his crow form then shifted back into his human one. "What's wrong?"

Ed motioned to Ann, who had just removed the last of Ceara's shackles.

"Holy crap!" Jax exclaimed and raised his staff. Light flowed around him as he hardened his skin and prepared for a possible attack.

"Stand down!" Ann said she rose to her feet. "No one is killing her."

"Jax, keep an eye on the Gliss."

Ed grabbed Ann's arm and pulled her aside. "Ann, we can't have a Gliss travelling with us. Especially not after everything she's done. She'll lead Urien straight to us." He kept a grip on her arm.

Why is she even suggesting such a thing? Jax asked.

Ed conjured a mental wall so Ann wouldn't overhear them. *Your guess is as good as mine.*

"She's not in any fit state to run off. She needs help." Ann tossed away the metal cuffs.

"Why would you help a Gliss? You hate them as much as anyone," Ed said. "Surely you can't trust her. Her wanting to help us is ridiculous. Look what happened the last time we trusted her."

"She helped me escape when Urien held me captive." Ann pulled her arm away from him. "She hates him."

"That doesn't make her an ally."

"She and I were friends once. She used to be your *sister*."

He glowered over at Ceara. "Yes, that's what makes her betrayal all the worse. She's the reason why I got turned into a beast. Gliss are incapable of being benevolent. They revel in pain and torture," Ed said. "I don't know why you'd even consider taking her with us."

"Xander asked me to help her. And after everything she showed me when I was held prisoner, I trust her. She doesn't need to prove her loyalty for me."

His eyes narrowed. Ed knew she'd had dreams Xander since Urien had possessed him. Even he couldn't believe Xander would suggest such a thing, not after Ceara had cheated on him with Urien. Ed knew the dreams were probably just a trick sent by Urien. No doubt he'd just be toying with his sister's emotions to manipulate her.

"That could be Urien posing as Xander, trying to trick you into taking pity on her," he said. "Urien must have known we'd come here. He'll use her to spy on us with."

"I know the difference between my brothers." Her brow creased.

"Orla tricked you into telling her how to free Urien's soul." He knew that was a low blow, but he had to make her see reason. They couldn't risk ever trusting Ceara again.

"I trust my instincts, and they are telling me to help her."

Sage came over. "I agree with the others. We can't have a Gliss with us," said the other druid. "Kill her. It was her kind who killed Flora. She should die."

Ceara glowered at Sage. "Of course you would blame me for Mum's death. I didn't kill Flora. I loved her; she was a mother to me." She made a move to get up again but stumbled back. She hit the ground, hard.

"Didn't do anything to save her, did you?" Sage snarled and pulled out a knife.

Ed's eyes widened. He'd never seen Sage threaten anyone before.

Ann gripped Sage's wrist. "Don't. Killing her wouldn't be what Flora would want."

Sage threw the knife to the ground in disgust and yanked her arm away from Ann. "How would you know what Flora would want? You didn't know her like I did. That bitch killed her." She jerked her hand at Ceara. "You are just letting her get away with it."

"I do know Aunt Flora loved her foster children more than anything. You'd be dishonouring her memory by killing Ceara. No one is going to kill her. That's an order. For all of you." She glanced from Ed to Jax then back at Sage. "Am I clear?"

Ed couldn't remember the last time she'd ever given them orders. *Guess she's more of the archdruid than she likes to let on. I knew the old Rhiannon Valeran was in there somewhere.*

"We need to get moving," he said. "Urien will sense something's wrong. We have a lot of ground to cover."

Ann drew a circle and traced different symbols on the ground. "Ed, help Ceara up, and everyone gather inside the circle." Ed opened his mouth to protest. "Just do it," Ann snapped.

Ed yanked Ceara up, and the five of them reappeared a few miles away in a large field full of dried grass and brambles. A ditch overgrown with nettles sat off to one side and a few large black horned cows sent curious glances their way. The scent of grass and nettles made Ed long for the smell of the sea again.

Ed's fangs ached to come out and hunt one of them down. *What is wrong with me? Damned beast.* He clenched his fists and yanked his leather fingerless gloves back on.

Ceara sagged against him, her legs unable to hold her up.

"There's a village not far from here. You and Jax go see if they have a healer." Ann rummaged through her pack. It looked like a plain leather satchel with a flap over it that fastened shut, but the bag had been charmed so it could hold an enormous number of items.

"I'm not leaving you and Sage alone with the Gliss." Ed crossed his arms.

She rolled her eyes. "Go, I'll be fine. Do you want me to make that an order too?"

"Ann, he's right," Jax said, gripping his staff. "We can't have a Gliss. She'll turn on us just like she did five years ago."

"Go, both of you," she snapped. "We're not going anywhere until Ceara's wounds are tended to."

Ed and Jax headed out to the nearby village of Mirstone. Grey stone houses with thatched rooves littered the cobblestone streets. The smell of vegetables and stew filled the air as they passed different stalls of merchants selling their produce.

He didn't like the fact they were still within the borders of Caselhelm, but Ann couldn't remain out of the land for too long without weakening. They always had to move around places on its border and remain one step ahead of Urien.

"Has Ann lost her mind?" Jax asked. "We can't have a Gliss with us. Not her. She'll kill us."

39

People called out to them, asking them to buy things. They couldn't afford to waste good coin on things they didn't need. Ed wanted to get to Trewa as soon as possible.

"I don't understand either." Ed shook his head. "She must feel sorry for her. Ceara helped her escape after Orla captured her and brought Urien back." He dodged a woman carrying buckets brimming with water. Some of it sloshed over his boots.

"She's still bloody Gliss!" Jax lowered his voice. "She betrayed us all once; what's to stop her from doing it again?"

"I know, but Ann is the archdruid. We can't—"

"I may have sworn fealty to her, but we don't have to take orders from her like we did with Darius. We're all friends, right?"

He shrugged. "Ann can and will pull rank when she wants to." He scanned the rows of houses. Up ahead was a set of small shops. All of them were tiny stone buildings with whitewashed walls and thatched roofs. Each one had a wooden sign hanging outside. More stalls surrounded them with people peddling their goods. "I should've mentioned about us wasting good coin too." Damn, why hadn't he thought of that earlier? Healers weren't cheap, and Ceara needed a lot of work done.

"Do you think she's gone a bit barmy after losing Xander?" Jax remarked. "After all she's been through, I wouldn't be surprised if she—"

"She's not mad. Maybe she's trying to fill the void left behind by Xander's absence." Ed eyed a stall selling fruit and bread. It would be worth stocking up on supplies.

"With a Gliss? They aren't exactly warm and cuddly people, brother."

"Let's just get this over with."

"Why can't we just tell her there's no healer here?" Jax grinned. "That way we wouldn't have to waste time or good coin on a healer. Maybe that will make her see reason."

"She'll know if we lie to her." Ed spotted the sign of an apothecary shop and headed inside. The shop appeared little more than one large room. The outside of it had walls that had turned grey with bits of white paint still showing underneath. Inside the room, the wooden floor was cracked and dirty. Shelves with different bottles, jars, and vials covered each wall, and different herbs hung from the wooden rafters. The air hung heavy with the smell from the different herbs.

The smell made Ed want to gag. He didn't like too many smells all at once. He took a deep breath, trying to get his senses to adjust to their new surroundings.

An old woman with weathered skin and washed-out blue eyes appeared behind the counter. "Good day to you. What can I help you with?" She wore a plain blue smock, and her grey hair was tucked underneath a black headscarf.

"We are looking for a healer," Ed replied. "Our…travelling companion is injured." He didn't think telling the truth would go over well. If Ann wanted a healer, he'd get her one.

"I'm an apothecary. I sell medicines, but I can help with minor injuries," she said. "Where is the person who needs tending to?"

Ed, you can't seriously be considering making this poor woman help Ceara, Jax said.

Ann told us to find help. That's what I'm doing.

"We need a healer, is there anyone here who can help with more serious injuries?" Ed asked, leaning against the counter. The scent of the herbs made his nose itch.

"The nearest healer is several miles away," she answered.

"How do you feel about working on a Gliss?" Jax remarked.

Jax, I never said to tell her the truth, Ed snapped.

The woman's eyes widened, and all colour drained from her face. "Get out, both of you," she hissed. "Don't come back."

Ed and Jax left. "Why did you mention she was a Gliss? If that woman spreads the word about Gliss being here, this place will be flooded with Urien's forces." He shook his head as they made their way back through the bustling marketplace.

"If no one will help, maybe Ann will see reason. You weren't going to leave Ceara here, were you?" Jax dodged out of the way of someone carrying two heavy buckets.

"No, we can't put innocent lives at risk. I thought maybe a healer would say she's too weak to travel and we could drop her off somewhere. We'll have to find another way to make Ann see reason.

CHAPTER 4

Urien let a scream of frustration as Xander's voice droned on inside his mind. *How much more of this must I endure?*

"My lord, is something wrong?" a Gliss named Olivia asked as she touched his arm.

He shoved her away so hard she hit the floor and rolled down the wooden steps of the dais. "Don't touch me," he hissed. "Someone report, have there been any signs of my father's vault yet?"

Olivia scrambled up. "What vault, my lord?" she asked, unsteady on her feet.

"*The* vault. I've told you worthless fools to find the vault!" he thundered.

Around him, the guards and two other Gliss all averted their gazes. They were used to his tirades and violent outbursts by now.

"Useless idiots," he growled.

See, even they doubt you. They might be afraid, but they don't respect you like a leader should be respected, Xander goaded. *Face it, you don't know who you are anymore.*

"What vault?" Olivia repeated. "We scanned the entire palace and found nothing."

Orla barged her way into the great hall. "You heard my son. Find the vault. It's not going to be lying around; it'll be sealed by magic." She moved to Urien's side. "Start looking for it. Now, get out, all of you."

Both the guards and the Gliss left without so much as a glance his way.

His fists clenched. "Who let you out?" he growled. "Don't order my people around like that. They answer to me now."

"Just as well I'm here. Look at you," she sneered. "You'll never convince anyone you're the archdruid. You're barely in control."

"Maybe you should've done your job and found my real body. Then I wouldn't be in this mess." Urien rocked back and forth.

Murderous bitch, Xander said. *She won't help you, brother. She has her own agenda planned. You'll never find Papa's vault either, because it doesn't exist.*

"What makes you think I trust you?" Urien snapped, still clutching at his head and grabbing fistfuls of his hair. No—not his hair. Xander's hair. Everything about this body felt wrong, alien to him. "This is my body. You're nothing more than memory."

Orla clutched his arm. "Stop listening to him. Drink the potion I made for you; it will help to silence him."

"I can't. He's always inside my mind."

"We'll find your body soon enough. Rhiannon won't leave her precious Xander to suffer." She gripped his shoulder. "You need allies, not just anyone. Time to reach out to the races that live beyond the mists. Remind them who the archdruid is."

Urien settled back on Darius's throne as Xander's voice fell silent for a moment. "I tried contacting the other elders. We need true power. I need allies if I'm to win over the five lands. They won't answer me, Mama." He rested his chin on his hand, sighing.

"I know. I fell out of favour with them because Darius died, but your siblings escaped. Our deal with them was for all the Valerans to die."

"How did Father know?" Urien asked. "He was *prepared*. That's why he cast that damned spell to protect me and my siblings from death. The bastard did it to stop me from killing them."

"Someone must've warned him. Probably that seer who told Rhiannon about the house of Valeran falling."

Urien remembered Ann coming to him. Telling him how a strange seer had predicted their family's demise. He'd kept her distracted by having a rogue sorcerer and ogres attack her. He'd hired an assassin to attack Darius as well, to make it look convincing. The man had failed. But it had been enough to keep everyone distracted whilst Orla and their people snuck into the palace on the night of the revolution.

Even Ann had seemed to believe the threat was over.

"Our goal is not to just gain allies, but to get the elders back on our side." Orla patted his shoulder. "Prove to everyone you're the archdruid and break through the mists. You have already taken Trin; the border mists are only a matter of time."

Urien picked up his goblet and gulped down the brew. The liquid burned the back of his throat. "Mama, this potion you made to repress Xander's spirit isn't working. You need to find a way to rid me of him." If he had to remain stuck in Xander's body, he would at least be the only occupant in it. The potion dulled his senses, but did little to mute Xander's annoying voice.

"When you find the vault, we'll have a way of solving all our problems, son." Orla smiled.

The doors to the great hall burst open as Constance stumbled in. Water dripped down her hair and face. Grass and dirt covered her leather bodysuit.

Urien rose. "What are you doing back here?" he demanded. "I told you to take control and stay on Trin until—"

"It's gone. The island is gone." Connie wiped her sopping wet hair off her face.

His eyes narrowed. "Gone? What do you mean?"

"Rhiannon and her rogues came. She sank the island and killed everyone stationed there," Connie said. "The island sank beneath the sea. She used her magic to do it. I escaped and used your transportation potion to get back here."

Urien's hands tightened into fists.

Xander laughed. *See, told you Ann's stronger than you.*

Quiet.

"An entire island can't just sink," Orla scoffed. "Even Rhiannon isn't that powerful."

"Rhiannon *could* do it. She's connected to Erthea, to nature as the archdruid." Urien gritted his teeth. "What about Ceara?"

"I left her to drown." Connie's lip curled. "No more than that traitorous bitch deserved."

Urien rose from his throne and took several strides across the hall. He grabbed the Gliss by the throat and lightning flared in his other hand. "Where is she? I told you to break her."

Connie's eyes widened in shock. "She…she…they saved her. One of them—the beast—tried to kill her. Rhiannon stopped him." Connie gasped. "They took her with them."

Urien pulled out one of the shock rods and pressed it to her throat. He channelled his own magic through it. Connie sank to her knees as volts of electricity shot through the cold metal of the rod. She screamed as the static rolled over her body.

Urien drew back. "Next time I give you an order, you'd better carry it out. I wanted Ceara alive." He kicked her in the stomach, then kicked her in the head. "Take her to the cells. I want her punished for her failure." He motioned for the guards outside to take away.

Urien stormed off to his private chamber. The room had once been Darius's office. It had a high vaulted ceiling, a huge fireplace, and empty shelves. Maps and a tapestry of Trin had once lined the barren grey stone walls. They'd all been stripped down after the revolution. Urien was determined to make this room his own.

All the books and maps were gone, but he'd already begun replacing them. A new map of the five lands hung over the fireplace. Caselhelm appeared in the most detail. Parts of Asral had been sealed off, and most of Lulrien had been lost to the toxic mists over the centuries. So mapmakers had been using the same images of the lost land for years to fill in the blanks.

Urien ran a finger over Trin. The druid isle looked like a tiny speck compared to Caselhelm, Asral, Gumorya, and Vala.

"Damn you, Rhiannon. Took one of the jewels in my crown, didn't you?" It didn't matter. Trin had been a small part of a much bigger puzzle he'd been building since his return.

It would take time to control all five lands as he intended. There were dozens of races and territories for him to conquer. Darius had controlled Caselhelm, the northernmost land, along with the icy mountains of Gumorya, and the desert land of Vala. Asral, the largest and most central land, had fallen in part to the former archdruid.

After two hundred years of rule, Darius had what Urien wanted. What he'd been promised when he made a deal with the elders.

Urien smiled. Even the beings of old despised his father as much as he had. Now, when he needed them most, they wouldn't come to him.

"Where were you going, sister? Most races won't help you because of the way former archdruids helped to enslave them," Urien said. "You can't leave Caselhelm for long. Gumorya is close, but its mountains are long and harsh. They fear you there too. Asral, then? There are many leaders there. You might even find an ally." He ran his fingers over the map. "Vala? No, the desert tribes never had much love for us Northerners either." He drew back from the map. "I don't have to find out. I have a spy in your midst."

He moved around his desk and picked up a scrying mirror. "*Taispeáin dom Ceara.*" Urien despised the ancient druid tongue, but the magic in him still responded to it.

The black glass shimmered, rippling over it like water in a pool as colour flooded through it.

The face of his sister stared back at him. Her long, wavy blond hair peeked out from the hood of her cloak. Urien didn't understand why she wore something so similar to the old Black's uniform. With her pale blue eyes and pale skin, she still looked as lovely as ever. Not beautiful in a traditional sense, but striking. She looked so much like their bastard father. More than Urien or Xander ever had. Urien guessed that was why Darius had favoured her most.

"We need to get you to a healer," Ann said.

So, Ceara is injured. Urien smile widened. *Good, that should slow them down enough for my men to track them.*

"I don't need a healer," Ceara insisted. "Where are we going?"

Ann rubbed something over Ceara's skin, no doubt to heal her wounds.

See. She saved Ceara, Xander remarked.

Fool, I wanted Ceara alive. The bitch has a tracking spell burned into her flesh. I wonder how long our dear sister will take to find it. Shut up.

49

"Somewhere safe," Ann replied.

Ed appeared. "We couldn't find a healer in the village," he told her, peeking into the tent.

Ah, my sister's ever faithful lapdog. Now, where are they headed?

"Did you even try to find one?" Ann rose to her feet.

"Yes. Jax told an apothecary we had a Gliss with us, so I doubt we'll find much help." Ed clutched the hilt of his sword. "We need to get moving. If we leave some supplies—"

"We're not leaving her. She's in no fit state to take care of herself," Ann snapped.

"I'm not an invalid." Ceara scowled at them.

"Get dressed. We've got a long journey ahead of us." Ann moved outside the tent.

Urien raised his hand to activate the spell he'd placed on Ceara. The skin on Ceara's neck flared with light and a spot on the map appeared above the fireplace.

Coleridge. Close to Trin. Or where Trin had once been.

So, my sister trusts you, Ceara, but not enough to tell you where they are going. No need, I can find you no matter where you go.

"Send out my sorcerers," Urien told the guard outside the door. "Tell them to follow my sister but not to get too close."

One way or another, he'd find that vault, and one by one, the lands would bow to him.

CHAPTER 5

Ann wasn't surprised when she heard the news that a healer wouldn't help them. She did feel annoyed Ed and Jax had told someone about travelling with a Gliss. She applied ointments to Ceara's wounds instead. She doubted they would do much good; Ceara still needed a real healer to treat any possible internal injuries.

She conjured one of their tents and got to work on checking over Ceara's injuries. Jagged burn marks covered her skin in different places where the magic from the shock rods had touched her. It made Ann shudder to think of the kind of torture Xander must have endured during his imprisonment before Orla had managed to put Urien's soul inside his body. The spirits only knew what he'd be enduring now at Urien's hand.

Ann cast a couple of healing spells anyway. Even if they only had limited effect, they might do some good. Too bad Gliss had a natural resistance to magic.

"I meant what I said," Ceara told her, wincing as Ann rubbed more ointment over her shoulders. "I want to help you in the fight against Urien. No matter what the others think. You helped me; I always repay my debts."

"You don't owe me anything," Ann replied. "And if we don't get you to a healer soon, you might not be fighting against Urien for very long."

Ceara snorted. "Are you joking? You were right about Urien. The bastard cast me aside for his new favourite, Constance. I stayed true to him all these years," she said. "You're the only one who can stop him." She flinched as Ann applied some healing balm to a wound on her forehead. "And I don't need a healer, I'll be fine. That stuff you're putting over me feels pretty good."

"It only numbs the pain and reduces the risk of infection. You need a healer to check you over. Your bruising could be masking internal injuries." Ann started reapplying the lids to the different jars. She had spent some time working in healing houses a few years earlier, when her mother was alive. Ann had never been trained as formal healer and only knew the basics of healing care. "Is that the only reason why you want to help us?" Ann shoved the vials back into her pack. "To get back at Urien?" She understood why the others were so distrustful of Ceara. But the Gliss had proved useful when she'd helped Ann escape from Urien's grasp.

Plus, Xander had asked her to help the Gliss, and she'd honour her brother's wishes.

Ceara shook her head. "No, Gliss are meant to serve the most powerful person—that's you," she said. "I'm tired of Orla's regime. I've been helping the resistance in secret for years. I wondered about what my life would be like if I hadn't chosen Urien. Now I'll find out." She winced as she sat up. "I'm still a Gliss—nothing will change that, but I swear fealty to you, Archdruid Rhiannon Valeran."

Ann's eyes widened. She hadn't expected that. An oath of fealty was binding. Like the vows the Black had made to her father. "I accept, but you need some new clothes. You can't travel in those things. I have—"

"I need my leather bodysuit," Ceara insisted. "They took it from me. No doubt you have one somewhere in that bag of yours. I know you've pretended to be a Gliss before; you broke into one of our temples."

"Maybe I do, but dressing as a Gliss will only make people warier of you." Ceara would stick out too much if she dressed like a Gliss. Ann, Ed, Jax, and Sage all had glamour spells disguising their true appearances. It made it much easier for them to blend in. They couldn't afford to stick out whenever they went anywhere. They needed to blend, to look like ordinary travellers without arousing any suspicions.

"I'm not ashamed of what I am. Now, unless you want me to walk around half-naked, give me the suit."

Ann fumbled inside her bag. She yanked out the brown leather suit and handed it to Ceara. "I'll be outside. Do you think you can walk? Do you need help dressing?"

"I'm sure wolfy could carry me, which would be more fun. But I'll manage."

Ann headed outside, where Sage rounded on her. "Have you lost your mind?" she hissed. "We can't have her with us. It's like giving Urien a beacon to follow us with."

"I'll use her to learn everything I can about Urien. She knows things about him that I don't," Ann said. "She can stay with us for now. If she tries anything, I'll deal with it."

Sage threw up her hands in exasperation. "Rhiannon, be reasonable. The Gliss are our enemies. She'll kill us the first chance she gets. You shouldn't be blinded out of some sense of childhood loyalty to her. She betrayed everyone when she had an affair and chose Urien. You seem to have forgotten about that. She fought on the enemy's side the night your parents were murdered."

Ann winced at the mention of her parents' murder. "I haven't forgotten about that. Just give Ceara the chance to prove she is different now. Let's get moving." She turned away from the other druid.

Ceara emerged from the tent dressed from head to toe in brown leather. The suit covered her from the leather corset that covered her torso down to her black leather boots and gloved hands. She still looked every inch a Gliss.

"Well, at least she looks the part now," Jax remarked, gripping his staff a little tighter.

"Ann—" Ed began.

She held up a hand to silence him. "You've already told me how you feel about her. Let's get moving. We've got a long way to go on foot," she said. "We'll see if we can get new horses along the way."

They'd lost their other horses during their escape from the palace in Larenth and hadn't had a chance to purchase any more yet. Moving around so much, they had to be careful how much coin they spent. Ann, Ed, and Xander had taken on jobs when they could in the past. Most of the time it was easier and cheaper just to walk or transport themselves to different places. Whatever horses they did manage to buy never seemed to last very long. Either the poor creatures suffered during their incessant battles or they just had to leave them behind.

"Where are we going?" Ceara asked, brushing her long black hair off her face. The only good thing the suit did was to cover up most of her extensive bruising and burns.

"That's not your concern," Ed retorted. "You're also not have any weapons while you're with us, is that clear?"

Ann saw the former guard and protector in him shining through. "He's right," she agreed. If it kept the others at ease, she wouldn't allow Ceara to be armed. Even injured, Ann suspected Ceara could still take care of herself without the use of any weapons.

Ceara frowned. "How am I supposed to defend myself?" She put her hands on her hips.

"I'm sure you can kill people with your bare hands." Sage shuddered, giving the Gliss another glare. "Let's go."

Ed and Jax went to the village and got five new horses from there—since Sage couldn't continue on foot and Ceara still had injuries—two black stallions and three mares. One mare was grey, the other two were a mix of black and white. Ed tied Ceara's horse to Jax's and told him to kill Ceara if she made any wrong moves—despite Ann's orders.

That annoyed Ann, but she knew it would take a while for both men to trust their foster sister again. She only hoped they could learn to. Travelling with them and Ceara bickering all the time wasn't going to be a very pleasant experience.

They made their way across the planes. Expanses of open grassland stretched out before them, where land and sky seemed to meet in the middle. It felt good to be away from any crowded villages or being stuck in one place. But being so out in the open with barely more than a few trees and a scattering of cows in the distance made Ann uneasy. Out here, they were visible to any potential attacks.

"What has Urien been up to since his return?" Ann asked Ceara and detached Ceara's mare from Jax's stallion.

"I have been imprisoned, remember?" Ceara remarked. "I haven't learned much of anything over the past month. Urien kept me locked up and the other Gliss tried to break me."

"Even prisoners hear things." Ed glowered at her. "Urien trusts you; he must've mentioned something about his plans. He always did like to gloat about things."

Ceara's dark eyes flashed. "He doesn't trust me anymore. I betrayed him by helping all of you, remember?" She tightened her grip on her reins. "He's been trying to gain new allies, some of Orla's men proved too weak for him. He's been trying to find other magic users too—people he can use. If they refuse, he kills them. Better to have them onside than to have other potential enemies."

"What about Xander?" Ann asked her. "Do you know if his spirit is still inside Urien's body? Does he have any control over his body?" Her heart pounded at the thought of her brother, and her stomach twisted with guilt.

Ed gave her a disapproving look. *She might only say what she thinks you want to hear.* Ann ignored him.

"It's horrible seeing Urien staring out through Xander's eyes. He even moves like Urien now." Ceara shuddered. "I think he's still in there. Urien looks like he's struggling at times, as if he can hear a voice no one else can. So I'd say yes, Xander is still alive. I doubt he has any control over his body."

The thought gave Ann a little comfort at least. If she could get Urien's spirit out, she could destroy him and save Xander at the same time.

They travelled the rest of the day, across the plains.

Ann remembered travelling over them as a teenager with her father. There had been a lot of druid settlements back then, and she'd enjoyed visiting them all. But most were gone. It was surprising how much places could change in only a decade.

She kept her senses alert as they moved. Ann had no doubt Urien's forces would be trying to follow her. Since she'd refused to join him, he'd want to find a way to kill her now. Or use her for his own means.

Darkness hung over them like a diamond filled blanket. Ann noticed Sage drooping in her saddle. "We should make camp for the night." Ann dismounted and pulled one of the tents out from her pack. She only had two tents. One she shared with Sage and one Jax and Edward slept in. Each tent had been created with magic and was made from wooden posts, along with a large canvas that covered the structure.

"I'm not sharing a tent with a Gliss," Sage announced as Ann set the tent on the ground and used magic to construct it.

Jax raised his hands. "Don't look at me either. I'm not sleeping anywhere near her." He gave Ceara a glare. "You might try to kill me."

"Why, afraid the big bad Gliss will come torture you in your sleep, bird boy?" Ceara scoffed. "You always were a coward. For the record, I don't plan on killing anyone. I want to get some sleep."

"I'd take your head off if you tried." Jax glared back at her. "And don't call me bird boy. That always used to annoy me when we were children."

"Jax, you can sleep in my tent," Sage said. "I would prefer to have someone near me who will kill a Gliss." Sage ducked inside the tent.

"Fine by me," Jax said. "Won't have you tossing and turning all night, Ed." He vanished inside the tent. He reappeared a few seconds later. "On second thought, someone needs to keep an eye on her and be ready for when Urien's people attack us." Jax motioned toward Ceara. Black light blurred around his body as he shifted into his crow form and hopped on top of the tent.

Ann repressed a sigh and pulled out a spare set of blankets from her pack. "Here, you should get some rest." She handed them to Ceara.

"I'm going for a walk," Ed said. "I'll sleep outside if I have to. Jax, you keep first watch."

Ann put her hands on her hips. "Ceara isn't our prisoner. You don't need to watch over her."

"She isn't our ally either." He stalked off without saying another word.

Ann tossed a few pieces of wood on the ground then threw a fireball at it to create a small fire. The flames erupted to life, sending shadows dancing across the hard ground.

Ceara made a makeshift bed with the blankets next to the fire and settled down. "You don't need to stick up for me," she murmured. "Nor can you expect them to trust me again so easily. I'll have to earn their trust back. That's my job, not yours."

"I know, but luckily, I do trust you." She pulled a couple of jars out of her pack. "Here, rub these on your skin if you need them. Hopefully there will be a healer who can help you where we're going." She still hadn't told Ceara of their exact destination and knew she couldn't keep a secret forever.

"*Sciath agus cosaint. Rabhadh faoi chontúirt.*" Ann set boundary spells for protection and to warn of any unwelcome visitors. Bursts of green light flashed around the perimeter of their camp, sending out tiny orbs as the wards set in place.

Pulling her cloak tighter, she followed after Ed. He stood staring up at the stars and seemed lost in thought. "Are you okay?" Ann asked, touching his shoulder. "You've been on edge all day."

"With a Gliss around, you can't blame me for that," he muttered and shrugged off her touch.

"That's not what's bothering you," she said. "Come on, talk to me."

He grunted something she couldn't make out.

"You're struggling to control the beast, but that doesn't mean you have to leave." Ann needed him to stay. He'd been part of her family for a long time. She knew him better than anyone.

"I can barely contain it. It gets worse every day," he said, scowling at the night sky. "I need it gone. I want to be myself again."

"Ceara, can you do anything to help Ed with his beast?" Ann called over to her. "To get rid of it?"

Ceara snorted. "You were born beast, wolfy." She pulled her blankets over her tighter.

Ed's jaw tightened. "That's not true. You changed me into it."

The Gliss turned and sat up, glaring over at him. "Really? I watched Orla torture you. It took us days before we finally brought out your true nature." She pulled her blankets up higher. "Face it, Ed. You've always been different. You know that. Even Mum said you weren't a druid, no matter how much you tried to act like one."

"Why would I even believe you?" he growled. "I remember what you did to me. Don't expect me to forgive you for the torture you put me through."

Ceara shrugged. "Believe what you like, wolfy. Do you remember your life before you washed up on Trin?"

Ed stalked off and Ceara burrowed under her blankets.

Ann hurried after him. "Would it really be so bad if you were born beast?"

He frowned. "How can you even ask me that?" he demanded. "I'm nothing like myself anymore. The beast wants nothing more than to hunt and kill. It wants blood, and it's taking everything in me to hold it back."

"Maybe I can help. My father taught me ways to hold my power in—that's how I kept my true power hidden all these years."

"How?"

"Meditation. It helps me to stay focused. It's a starting point at least." Ann took off her cloak and laid it out on the ground. "Sit down. Let's try something. Maybe it will get you to relax."

The others were a good distance away so they wouldn't disturb them. She only hoped Jax didn't try to pick a fight with Ceara whilst they were gone.

"I can't relax—not with a Gliss lying a few feet away."

"Do you trust me?"

"Of course. I trust you with my life."

"Good, then trust my judgement and stop obsessing over Ceara." She motioned to the ground. "Lie down." She settled down on her cloak, ignoring the pebbled ground underneath the leather.

Ed sighed and sat down beside her. "What do you want me to do?"

"Just relax. I'll cast a spell of calmness. Maybe that will make things easier to control. Close your eyes."

"You know my beast seems to be immune from magic. Gliss magic doesn't work against me, so yours may not work either," he pointed out as he settled down beside her.

"It will if you let the magic work. Just don't resist me." Ann took his hands and drew magic. *"Calma agus a bheith fós."*

Her fingers tingled, and Ed gripped her hands tighter. Their minds opened to each other. There had always been a strong link between them, ever since they were children. No one had ever been able to explain their natural connection to each other. The link had always been there. Neither of them had ever questioned it. It was just part of them.

Ann felt the beast at the edge of his mind, clawing and trying to break free. Ed had constructed a cage around it, locking it inside. The beast felt powerful, strong…and angry. It wanted freedom. Darkness seeped from it too. It didn't feel evil—just primal. She couldn't see the creature itself, or any kind of light around it. That led her to believe it was a natural part of him and not an intruding entity. If it were, she would have sensed that by now.

Ann repeated the spell to it, and it snarled, shaking off the magic like an irritation. This time she focused on Ed himself.

Ed drew away once the spell ended. "Guess I feel a little better." He wrapped his hands around the back of his head and laid back on the ground. "Thanks. I hope it helps."

"I think your beast is immune to spells," Ann remarked. "Maybe you should look on it as a gift."

"A gift?" Ed scoffed. "How can it ever be a gift?"

"You're stronger and more powerful now than you were." He'd always been the strongest out of all the Black.

"I might be able to rip people's heads off and be fast, but I can't even use magic," he said. "Not even the basic things. I feel like I've lost myself."

"Maybe it's time for a change. I never thought I'd be a rogue druid, yet here I am, the archdruid."

"I hate feeling like I don't know myself anymore."

Ann flopped back against the grass, rested her head against his shoulder. "You'll learn about the beast and who you are. Maybe it's time to find out more about who you were before you came to Trin."

"That's never mattered to me. Flo was my mother. Your family was there for me," he said and sighed. "I still miss Flo. I can't believe she's gone." He pushed his long hair of his face. "Where I came from isn't important. I'm not sure I want to know."

Ann winced at the mention of Flora. Her heart twisted thinking of her aunt. Flora had been just another one of the victims in Urien's war against them. "I know, I miss her too. I think she would want us to give Ceara another chance."

Ed gritted his teeth. "You don't know that."

She arched an eyebrow. "No? Flora was one of the most forgiving people I've ever known. She believed in second chances more than anything." Ann turned her head to stare back up at the glittering night sky. Watching the stars had always been something they'd done together as children, and it felt good to be doing it again now. "The other druids might be able to help."

"You can't really be considering taking Ceara to Trewa with us?"

She bit back a smile. *I wondered how long it'd be before he brought that up.*

"No one trusted you when you washed up on Trin—an island hidden by magic and only accessible to druids," Ann pointed out, giving him a playful nudge in the ribs.

"I wasn't a Gliss. I was just a kid who had no idea where he came from or who he was," Ed said, turning his body to face her. "Why do you want to save her so much?"

"Because she was one of us once. We were friends, and she was your sister."

Ed rolled his eyes. "Once. She still betrayed us. She chose Urien above her own family." He brushed bits of grass off his trousers. "People can't change that much. You wouldn't expect Urien to change after all the evil he's done, would you?"

Ann winced. She had always wondered if Urien would change. Despite all the bad things he'd done, he'd been her brother. "No," she admitted. "I believe people can change if they want to, and I think Ceara does." She squeezed his shoulder. "Just like I know you can learn to control your beast."

Ann woke with the sun hanging overhead and birds singing. Bright orange rays filled the pale blue sky. A chill wind washed over her skin. She blinked and realised she'd fallen asleep with her body half-draped over Ed's.

"Some things never change." Ceara loomed over them, smiling.

Ann wriggled free of his grasp and sat up. "What do you mean?" She pushed her long hair off her face and rubbed sleep from her eyes.

A quick glance at Ed revealed his eyes were still closed. She doubted he was still asleep with Ceara so close to them.

"You and Ed. Well, at least you found someone who actually loves you," Ceara said and scowled. "Unlike Urien."

"We're not a couple." Ann brushed dust off her clothing. She tugged on her cloak, trying to pull it up, yet Ed still lay over half of it, so she couldn't.

Ceara rolled her eyes. "And you're still denying it even after all these years."

"It's the truth," Ann insisted.

"Right, keep telling yourself that." Ceara laughed

Ed bolted up. "Someone's coming." He scrambled for his sword, which made Ann arch an eyebrow at him. Although he'd been carrying his sword around for the past few months after changing into a beast, he hadn't used it very often. Then again, maybe he didn't want to unleash his beast unless he had to.

Ann glanced around, seeing only Jax and Sage sitting around a small fire over by their tents. "Where?"

"Close. I can hear them." He unsheathed his sword with a hiss.

Ceara tensed beside them. "I need a weapon. Ed, give me your sword. You don't need it."

"Not a chance, and yes, I do need it," Ed replied.

A flash of orange light came at them. Ceara raised her hand and deflected the blast.

Nice way to wake up in the morning, Ann thought as heat flared between her fingers.

CHAPTER 6

Ed felt his beast clawing to get out now it caught the scent of magic and the hint of battle in the air. It wanted out. He struggled to keep it under control. Instead, he gripped his sword. Maybe using that instead of unleashing his inner beast would help keep the creature reined in.

More blasts of orange light came at them.

One grazed the side of his face with a sting of heat.

He narrowed his eyes, spotted a group of men heading their way. "There's five of them. Sorcerers," he told the others.

"Sage, stay in the tent," Ann said.

Sage snorted as she got up. "I'm not without my uses." The druid brushed off her robe and light flared between her fingers as she prepared herself for battle.

Jax drew his staff. "Urien's people?"

"Guess we're about find out."

The men came at them from all directions.

Ed lunged at the first sorcerer. A bolt of energy hit his shoulder. Smoke seared through his shirt and jerkin. He raised his sword as another blast of energy came at him. The metal flashed as the magic bounced off, absorbed by the steel. One good thing about this weapon was it had been made from steel infused with magic. All of the Black had been given weapons capable of fighting and absorbing magic. The blade felt familiar in his grasp, almost as if it was part of his own body.

The first sorcerer, a rotund man with a balding head and beady black eyes, drew back as Ed advanced toward him. The man pulled out a knife; it shook within his trembling hand as Ed swung the blade at him.

The knife fell from the man's grasp. He raised his hand, throwing another bolt of energy at Ed. The bolt bounced off his sword as he grabbed the man by the throat.

Inside his mind, the beast thrashed and growled, demanding to be let out. It wanted blood. This sorcerer's blood. Ed's hands shook as his claws tried to come out.

"Who sent you?" Ed growled, squeezing the man's throat so hard his eyes bulged.

The smell of the man's fear only excited his beast more. He gripped his sword harder with his free hand in an effort to keep it in.

Kill, the beast demanded.

The sorcerer opened his mouth to speak and coughed. No words came out. His heart pounded wildly as he fought for air.

Ed let go of the man, gripping his sword so tight the metal on the hilt twisted in his grasp. His eyes flashed emerald. His upper jaw ached for his fangs to come out.

The sorcerer doubled over, gasped for air. Another man with long dark hair came at Ed from the side. The second sorcerer raised his dagger, about plunge it into Ed's neck. Ed spun and knocked the dagger away with one swipe of his sword, the blade flashing with silver light as he moved. He thrust his sword through the man's chest in one fell swoop. The second man's eyes widened in shock as blood gurgled from his mouth.

Ed shoved the body away as he drew his sword back and swung at the other sorcerer, dispatching him in the same manner as the second one. He took a deep breath, leaning on his sword. The fingerless gloves strained as his claws flashed over his fingers. *Damn it, no. I'm in control. Not you.*

He searched his memories, trying to remember the words to the spell Ann had used on him the night before. But they wouldn't come to him. Not here, in the midst of battle with blood pounding in his ears and adrenaline racing through his veins.

Ed turned his attention back to the others.

Ann muttered words of power and sent another man crashing to the ground. The sorcerer struggled to get up, throwing another bolt of energy straight at her. Ed deflected it with his sword, the blade flashing as he blurred to her side.

"Are you okay?" she asked.

He gave her a curt nod. Better not to let her know how much he was struggling. It would only distract her, and he couldn't afford to do that. Not at a time like this.

Jax swung his staff as one of the other men came at him. Orange flashed light around him as he hardened his skin, protecting himself.

"Don't kill them. I want to know who sent them," Ann called.

The beast growled, thrashing against the cage of his mind as it tried to take full control once more. *Out.* But Ed wouldn't let it. Not this time.

The beast didn't want to keep these men alive. It wanted to taste blood. Feel their bones crunch and break. Rip them apart.

No, I've got to stay in control. Ed flew at the sorcerer and grabbed the man by the throat. "Who sent you after us?" he growled, voice low and guttural. "Tell me, or you'll meet the same fate as your friends."

"Archdruid…" the man rasped. "Ordered it…"

Urien. He snapped the man's neck and dropped the body to the ground.

Ed turned and saw Ceara grab a man by the throat and begin to strangle him with his own magic. *And Ann thinks she's weak.*

Ed blocked another man as he came at him, and quickly dispatched him.

The beast growled, and his eyes flashed.

Sage raised her hand, calling up vines that wrapped around one man, and knocked him off his feet.

Ed felt his control slipping away once more. His fangs slipped out and his claws emerged. His sword fell from his grasp, clattering to the ground.

Ann blasted two other men and Jax sliced the remaining two.

The last sorcerer caught in Sage's vines tried to crawl away. The vines held him in place. He called out to his fallen comrades to help. But they were all dead now.

Ann raised her hand and power crackled around in a glowing dome of white energy as she trapped the sorcerer within a ward. "Ed, come back. Now," she said.

His fists clenched. "I can't," he growled.

"Yes, you can." Ann made a move toward him, but he backed away.

"Stay away!" His eyes flashed with light.

"Focus. Stop fighting it and calm your mind." She reached for him. Ed took another few steps away from her. He wouldn't risk hurting her again. This time he might do far worse than knock her to the ground. Just because she couldn't die didn't mean she couldn't get hurt. He had enough blood on his hands already.

"Come on, Ed. Change back." Jax kept his staff drawn. No doubt ready to use it in case Ed tried to attack them.

Ann glanced at Ceara. "Can you help him?"

Ceara approached him. "Wow, you do look like a real beastie." She grinned. "See, you are stronger than you ever were before. Stop fighting it and control it instead. It's a gift. It's who you are. Fighting it will only make it harder for you."

He snarled. If the beast wanted blood, he'd give it some. His eyes flashed, and he lunged at the Gliss.

Ceara raised her hand, white light forming across her forehead as her power flowed free and her eyes widened. "What the...?"

Ed felt a rush of exhilaration. She couldn't use her abilities against him. Ceara dodged him as he made a grab for her. Power pulsed from between her fingers, her magic hit him like an oncoming storm. Ed shook his head, shaking off the feeling. "Your power is useless against me," he hissed.

Ann jumped between them, raising her hands. "Stop! I told you not to harm her," she said. "Would you hurt me instead?"

The beast didn't want Ann. It wanted Ceara. It wanted the traitor's blood. It remembered how she tortured him. Memories of pain, of his bones aching as they bent and broke flashed through his mind. The feel of a whip on his back and the stinging, burning sensation of a rod at his neck. She'd done this to him.

"Are you going to hurt me?" Ann asked. "If you want to get to her, you have to go through me." She lowered her hands to her side.

He snarled at her as he let out a low growl. "Don't come been between me and my prey."

Ann walked straight up to him, her face only inches from his. "Do you want to hurt me? Because that's what you have to do if you hurt her."

Ed halted, remembered how he'd loved the feeling of holding her earlier. He'd never wanted to let her go. No, he couldn't hurt her. How could he? She was a part of him, part of his own soul. Just as this beast was part of him.

All at once the beast retreated inside. Breathing hard, he wrapped his arms around her and pulled her close. To his relief, she didn't pull away. Instead, she returned his embrace as he buried his face against her shoulder for a moment. "Thanks."

Ceara breathed a sigh of relief. "Jeez, don't do that again," she muttered. "You'd learn some control if you didn't stop bloody resisting the beast all the time."

Ed ignored her, holding on to Ann a moment longer before pulling away. "Did you just bind that sorcerer?"

She arched a brow. "How did you know?"

"I felt it in the air. How did you do that?" He and Ann had grown up together. Ed knew what she could magically do. Binding someone through sheer thought wasn't one of them. Only Darius had been able to do that.

Ann shrugged. "I just did it." She moved over to the sorcerer, who knelt, frozen in place. "Who sent you?"

Ed moved to her side. "I'd answer her if I were you." He bent, retrieved his fallen sword, and wiped away the blood on the grass. Ed kept the blade within his grasp in case the sorcerer tried anything.

"I could get answers out of him," Ceara offered.

The man trembled. He appeared tall and slim, with a shock of black hair and blue eyes. "Please don't hurt me," he begged. "I-I'm just following orders. He said he'd kill our families if we didn't agree to track down the pretender."

"Pretender?" Jax frowned, leaning on his staff and the orange glow around his skin faded.

The man eyed Ann. "You. Urien says you're pretending to be the archdruid and you want to—"

Ann's eyes flashed with power, and the man tried to back away but couldn't. The binding still held him in place.

"I'm the archdruid. Urien is the pretender." She raised her hand. The man fell forward as the binding broke. "Take your family and leave," she said. "Get away from Urien. I won't be merciful if you attack me or my friends again."

The man scurried away, muttering a thank-you as he went.

"Why did you let him go?" asked Ceara. "He'll go running back to Urien and—"

"I don't kill people for the sake of it," Ann said. "I scanned his thoughts and sensed he told the truth. He was only trying to protect his family."

Ceara scoffed. "Urien will guess where you're going."

"Let him. I'm done hiding," Ann said. "Pack up. We need to get moving."

Ed tried to ignore the feel of the beast clawing at the cage of his mind. It still hadn't settled down after their last battle. "What do you know about this thing inside me?" he asked Ceara. "Why did Orla turn me into this?"

"I told you, Orla let it out. She didn't create it—although, believe me, she tried," Ceara replied. She knelt and gathered up her blankets in a messy bundle.

"Yeah, she tortured and killed most of the Black by turning them into beasts," Jax said as he shoved his canteen and some leftover food into his own pack. "Right after the revolution. They all died."

Ceara nodded, leaving the blankets in a pile as Ann and Sage dismantled the tents. "Orla wanted stronger, more powerful warriors for her armies. She planned on interbreeding them with Fomorian demons."

"Weren't the Gliss powerful enough?" Jax scoffed, taking a swig from his canteen. "You can kill someone with a single touch. And you can deflect magic when it's used against you."

Ceara shook her head and put her hands on her hips. "Gliss were Urien's creation. He helped us to be—"

"His harlots," Jax sneered and swung his pack over his shoulder.

Ceara glared at him. "Women withstand pain in ways men never can. That's why Urien taught us how to be stronger. Stronger than any other Magickind and use our gifts in a way they'd never been used before."

"What did Orla expect me to do?" Ed persisted. "I'd never serve her. She should know that." He still didn't remember much about those months he'd spent as a captive of Orla. He knew she tortured him and held him for three months until he'd somehow escaped and found his way back to Ann. Ed had had a few nightmares, but most of it remained blank.

"She thought your beast-like nature would destroy the humanity in you," Ceara said. "You were in a mindless rage for days—it surprised even Orla."

Ed tried to picture it, to remember what he'd gone through. Nothing came at him. All of it remained a blank. Strange, he'd remembered flashes of it during their battle earlier. Now, aside from a few snarls and growls, the beast remained silent inside the cage of his mind.

"How did Orla even know this beast was supposedly inside me?"

Ceara shrugged. "She didn't tell me everything. Guess she sensed it somehow." She glanced over at Jax as he helped Sage roll up one of the tents. "We always knew you were different. You were always stronger and faster than any of the Black."

What am I? Ed wondered. *Why is this thing inside me?* More questions buzzed around his mind, but no answers came to him.

"Did Orla know how to control it?" he asked.

The Gliss frowned, thoughtful. "I doubt it. She liked to pretend she was more knowledgeable than she was." She touched her chin. "Whatever Magickind you are, you must've come out of one of the other lands. Some parts of the five lands are either closed off with magic or cut off by the toxic mists left over from the dark times."

"Why are you really here?" Ed wanted to know. "Did Urien send you?"

Ceara's eyes narrowed. "Oh, sure, pester me with questions, then turn on me. You men are all the same. You use women to get what you want when it suits you. My reasons aren't your concern. I'm not a threat to Ann."

"Yes, you are, and the minute you make a wrong move—"

"Who is more dangerous to her?" Ceara crossed her arms. "Me or you? You can barely control yourself. I've seen the way you look at her. The beast in you wants her too, doesn't it?"

Ed muttered a curse under his breath and turned away from her. Better to end the matter now. If he grew angrier, he risked losing control again. Better to ignore Ceara anyway. Sooner or later, she'd reveal her true nature. He was sure of that.

Ann rolled up the tents and shoved them into her pack as she, Jax, and Sage headed over to the horses and climbed up into the saddles.

Ed grabbed the reins of his own mount, swung up into the saddle and urged his stallion forward to join Ann as she led the way with Sage riding close beside her.

"I need to know more about this thing inside me," he said Ann. "You can help me remember more about my life before I landed on Trin."

"We can try later." She swung her pack onto her back. "Ceara, do you know anything else about controlling the beast?"

"If you gave me a shock rod, I'm sure I could get it into submission."

Ed scowled at her. "You're not having any kind of weapon, much less using it on me." His hands tightened on the reins and his stallion snorted, uneasy. *Ignore her,* he told himself. *She's trying to get under your skin.*

"You'll need to create an alliance with the druids, too," Sage remarked as she rode up alongside Ann.

"I am a druid," Ann pointed out.

"Yes, you've been a fugitive for the past five years," Ed remarked.

"They might not be welcoming toward you. You'll have to regain their trust again." *And I'll have to keep it together myself.* He didn't expect a warm welcome from the druids either when they found out he was a beast.

He and Ann hadn't sought sanctuary among them in their years on the run due to Orla's spies being everywhere. Orla would have expected them to have gone to seek shelter among Ann's own people.

"The druids have been leaderless since your father's death, and Orla has killed a lot of them," Sage said. "I still kept in contact with your uncle over the years. The druid numbers are dwindling. Orla seemed determined to wipe our people off the face of Erthea." She grimaced. "Your uncle, Blaise, has led the people of Trewa for the past decade. He is well-respected and works hard to keep our people safe."

Ann scowled at the mention of her uncle's name. "I doubt they'll be very happy to see me."

"Remember, we need the druids on your side," Sage said. "Urien will be gathering to him any and all allies he can. You need your *own* allies, not just those among the resistance."

Ceara drew up closer to them, bickering with Jax as she went. He urged her to stay behind and seemed to want to keep a close eye on her. "Are we going to see the druids then?" Ceara asked, frowning when they all turned to stare at her. "What? I don't understand why you don't just tell me. I'm not going to go running and blabbing to Urien, if that's what you're worried about."

"Maybe not, but that doesn't mean we trust you." Jax grabbed hold of her reins. "Stay close don't try grabbing any weapons again."

After the others had settled down for the night later that day, Ed led Ann away from the camp. If they were going to go digging around for bits of his forgotten past, he didn't know how his beast would react. It would be safer for everyone if they didn't find out.

Ann drew a circle on the ground and put down protective runes. Each symbol glowed with fiery blue light. "Are you sure you want to do this?" she asked. "I don't know what kind of memories will come to the surface. It could dredge up your time of being imprisoned."

"I have to do this. I need to know if this thing is really part of me or not."

"And if it is?" Ann touched his shoulder. "I know—"

Ed shook his head. "Let's get started." He sat down in the circle.

He didn't care what memories rose to the surface. Ed just needed to know more about this thing that kept trying to take control of his body.

Ann sat down and took his hands. Her touch seemed to calm the beast, as it quietened at the edge of his mind. She chanted words of power and a breeze whipped through the circle.

Ed closed his eyes and the field around them faded. He reappeared sitting on the shores of Trin, staring at the tranquil waters of eastern sea. Its grassy embankments and the smell of salty air felt familiar to him. He felt at peace here, safe. This had been the first real home he'd ever known before he'd gone to live in Caselhelm. It was where Ann had found him.

Ann appeared beside him.

"I miss this place," Ed remarked. "Everything seemed so simple when I first came here. Not like now."

"Let's go back. What do you remember before that?" Ann said. "Let your mind wander. Back to before your life here, what you see?"

Ed hesitated. He'd never cared much about his missing past. It hadn't mattered. No one had ever come looking for him.

Images flashed as he found himself submerged by water. The current dragged him down as he kicked and thrashed, trying to get back toward the surface. His lungs burned for air as he tried to get his head back above the water. The blackness of the water enveloped him like a heavy cocoon. Flashes of light danced above his head. In his mind, he felt another presence. *Is that the beast?* It felt different here in his memories. Not harsh and primal as it was in his waking life.

Ed coughed, reappearing back on Trin. "That doesn't tell me anything."

"I told you, you can't predict what will come to the surface. What else do you see?"

Trees flashed by, branches catching his clothes as he remembered being a boy. Something or someone chased him. Blood pounded in his ears as his heart raced. Unfamiliar scents assaulted his senses. Yet they seemed strangely familiar.

Magic hissed on the air like a hungry bloodhound chasing him, trying to find him.

When he reached the edge of the river, he jumped in. The current caught hold of him and pulled him away.

"You can't run forever, boy. I will find you," a voice called after him.

Ed opened his eyes, breathing hard. He found himself back in the field. The sky above him appeared like a blanket of darkness. Not a cloud or star in sight. "Something chased me. Someone with magic."

Ann sagged against him. "That took a lot more power than I expected."

He wrapped an arm around her as she rested her head against his shoulder. He wanted to go back in and find out more, but not at the expense of hurting her. "At least I've had a glimpse of my past. Do you want me to help you back to camp?"

"No, stay here." Her eyelids drooped. "Sorry I can't help more."

He laughed and pulled her closer. *You have no idea how much help you are to me.*

Her closeness seemed calm the beast again, and his heart ached with unspoken feelings. Now he'd finally glimpsed part of his missing childhood, but he still had no idea what it all meant.

CHAPTER 7

Ann spotted Xander in the gloom around her. To her relief, the spell had worked and taken her into the blackness of limbo. Darkness fell around her like a heavy blanket, creeping with silvery tendrils of mist. There were no buildings here. No life. Nothing substantial.

"You're here." She threw her arms around him, but his form flickered. "By the spirits, I miss you so much. Are you alright?" It felt good just to see him again, to feel his familiar presence.

"I'm trapped inside my own body, Annie. How can I be alright?" Xander asked and took a step back. "Urien knows you're going to Trewa."

"That's no surprise." She sighed. "He'd know it's the first place I'd go to." She stared at him. "What has he been doing?" Ann knew she didn't have a lot of time. As much as she wanted to stay here and talk to him, she couldn't waste the precious seconds they had together. "What's he planning to do next? I need you to tell me everything you know."

"Gathering allies. Trying to build his forces," Xander said. "Is Ceara with you?"

Ann hesitated. She believed this was her brother's spirit, but she'd been tricked before. "Ceara escaped from Trin," she admitted. "Urien sent sorcerers after me."

"He's terrified you'll find a way to banish him again." Xander smiled. "I enjoy watching him being scared. Strange, I never thought him capable of fear when we were children. He never acted like anything scared him."

Xander seemed to have a hardness in his eyes she's never seen before. *By the spirits, don't let Urien change him. He is one of the few good things I have left in my life.*

"I'm working on a way of saving you—I will save you," she promised. Ann reached out to touch him again, then drew. "I wish I could touch you. I'm doing everything I'm can to stop him."

"Urien is stronger now he has my power combined with his own," Xander said. "You should be focused on stopping him, not saving me. There has to be a way around Papa's curse to make sure he can die. Even if it means killing me, too."

Her eyes widened. "Don't say that." She couldn't understand how he could say that. How could he even think that?

Xander's jaw tightened. "I mean it, Ann. Stopping Urien is more important than my life. Don't waste your energy on saving me. All your effort should be focused on stopping him. There is too much at stake not to do that."

"Not to me, it's not!" she snapped. "How can—?"

"You know I'm right. Urien will kill hundreds of people. If you can stop that, you have to," he said. "Find a way to undo the spell that binds us together. It's the only way to stop him."

"But you could die," Ann protested. "How can you ask me to do that? You're one of the few surviving family members I have left."

"I trust you to do the right thing. Deep down, you know I'm right."

Ann dragged herself out of the dream as she opened her eyes. Tears dripped down her cheeks and her chest tightened. She rarely cried anymore. She thought she'd lost the ability after grieving for her parents for so long. Yet seeing Xander and talking to him broke her heart.

Ed's arms snaked around her. "What's wrong?"

"Xander told me to break the spell that binds my siblings and I together." She sniffed. "Even if it means…" She couldn't get the last words out.

"We'll find a way to save him." He pulled her closer, tightening his embrace.

Ann clung to him. He'd always been there when she needed him. He'd been her rock through everything.

But she knew when he said things she wanted to hear. Reluctantly, Ann pulled free of his arms and sat up. "Even a reversal spell might not be enough. I still need Urien's soul out of Xander's body," she said. "I won't kill Xander just to stop him."

She didn't know if reversing their father's spell to cheat death would even be a possibility. The magic he had used had been beyond anything she knew herself. It could take months to figure out a spell, then even longer to find a way to reverse it, if it could be reversed at all.

Finding the vault and locating the spell Darius had used on them would be the first step. If she could reverse it, Ann would, but not at the expense of Xander's life. One way or another, she'd save him.

Ed sat up beside her. "Maybe your uncle can help. He knew your father better than anyone, including things about his magic."

Her lip curled at the mention of Blaise. "He won't be happy to see me. You know we never got along very well." She dreaded the thought of seeing her uncle again. He and Darius had never been close. Ann had no idea how he would react to her arrival or what he would do. She might be the archdruid in name and power, but Blaise had led their people for over five years now.

Ed brushed her hair off her face. "You are the archdruid. You have it in you to be it."

Her heart clenched at his last words. She never wanted to be the archdruid. Back before her father's murder, part of her had hoped he'd go on ruling as he done for the past two centuries. Being the archdruid gave longevity and good health. If Urien hadn't killed him, would Ann have ever become the archdruid at all? She always wanted to follow her own path, not to be dictated by the rules of the past or by people's expectations. In a horrible way, Darius' death had given her just that.

His fingers felt warm against her skin and their eyes locked for a moment. Ann turned away, uneasy by the feeling. "Just like I know you can control your beast."

Ed let out a low growl. "That's not the same. You were born to be the archdruid."

"Urien is older than me," she pointed out. "If he had been born with the power, he could have easily become the archdruid. Not me. I sometimes wonder why he didn't. I always wondered what things might have been like if Urien had been the heir instead. Would he have turned out different?"

"Urien is a bastard with demon blood. You are Darius's true heir." Ed's jaw tightened. "Don't question that. Urien would've been a terrible leader. He would've been just like the stories of the archdruid of old. Cold, vindictive. Ruled by power. The five lands and the rest of Erthea have suffered enough of that over the centuries. Now it's finally time for a change."

"Maybe. Maybe not." She sighed, knowing there was no point dwelling on what might have been. The past couldn't be changed. "Is it really that different? You could have been born a beast," she said. "Maybe you just didn't know it."

"Perhaps. If this is a curse I'm under, I will find a way to break it."

Ed helped her up and they headed back toward the camp.

They set out after a quick breakfast the next morning. The sun rose, casting its golden rays over the horizon. A chill wind bit across her skin, and Ann pulled her cloak tighter as she climbed up into the saddle. Another day of hard riding would finally lead them to their destination. She had mixed feelings about getting to Trewa. How would the druids even react to her arrival? Would they be glad to see her, or had the days of respecting the archdruid long passed?

"I haven't been to Trewa since before my father died," Ann said to Sage. She didn't see the point in trying to hide their destination from Ceara anymore. The Gliss already knew where they were going. "How many druids are left there?"

"About a hundred during my last visit," Sage replied.

Ann's eyes widened. "So few?" She had known Orla had been dead set on wiping out her father's people. A few years earlier there had been at least a thousand druids left at the settlement. How could so many have died in such a short time?

Her hands tightened into fists. *Damn it, I should've been here for them. Instead, I spent all these years on the run.*

"How did a druid settlement even survive?" Ed asked. "Orla declared war on the druids after the revolution."

"Trewa is protected by the standing stones," Sage explained. "Their power has kept the place safe for generations. No one has been able to breach that. Too bad more of them didn't stay there."

"I thought only the archdruid could channel their power," Ann remarked, remembering what her father had taught her about the place.

"The Gliss have tried to take Trewa more than once," Ceara said as she rubbed another balm over her bare arms. She'd taken off the top half of the bodysuit and now just wore a corset over a loose black tunic. "The druids fight hard. I always admired that."

Ann glanced over at her. She'd wanted to examine Ceara's wounds again, but Ceara had refused, insisting she'd be fine.

"Yeah, and the Gliss fight harder," Jax muttered.

Ann had noticed Jax seemed more uncomfortable around Ceara than the others. She suspected it was from the time he'd been imprisoned by Orla. Unlike Ed, Jax remembered what the Gliss had done to him. Or perhaps it was just uncomfortable for him to have his foster sister around again. From what she remembered, Jax had rescued Ceara from the streets as a baby, then Flo had taken them in.

Ann felt a pang of guilt. She didn't want to upset her friends. Jax might have only come back into her life a few weeks earlier, but he'd always been loyal. It had been good to find one of the Black still alive—for both her and Ed.

Ed had been by her side through everything, both in her life as Rhiannon Valeran and now as the rogue archdruid.

"We should be on our guard. I don't know how my uncle or the other druids will react to me being there," she said, relieved they should finally reach Trewa later that day.

As they rode, Ann scavenged through her memories of spells. Her dream about Xander only made her all the more determined to save him.

She searched through things she hadn't thought about in years. If she could use a strong unlinking spell and work some complicated runes into it, it would be a start, at least.

Ann knew she couldn't wait around to find the vault. She had to work fast on a spell to get Urien's spirit out of Xander's body.

When they stopped to let the horses rest, Ann drew runes on the ground. "*Gan aon fhuil a cheangal.*" Fire flashed around her circle, then it exploded in a violent burst of energy.

Damn, I'm a little rusty, but that should have worked!

"I used to be good at this," she muttered.

"You still are." Ed appeared beside her. "You're just out of practice."

"Didn't have much of a choice whilst we were running from Orla for the past few years." Ann hated not being able to use the full extent of her powers but had grown used to it. She'd need all her power to stop Urien and save Xander.

Ann closed her eyes, tried again. Still nothing. The others all stood bickering with Ceara. The noise faded and she heard Ed say something about going hunting with Jax.

"*Seó a leanann.*" She muttered a spell as she stared down into the water to see if anyone was following them. The water shimmered. Something flew at her from behind, knocking her back against the hard ground.

A skeletal beast with glowing red eyes hovered over her, pinning her arms down with its front paws. Its body appeared to be the skeleton of a cat-like animal. Its hollow eye sockets glowed with eerie light. No fur covered it.

A knife came out of nowhere and embedded itself in the

creature's side. The blade lodged in the its ribs. The creature hissed and scurried away.

Ceara came over and gave her a hand up. "We need to move," the Gliss said. "That was a scout. A horde of banelings will be swarming through here soon." She picked up the discarded knife.

"Banelings? I thought they were just a myth," Ann remarked.

"They are. But things still come through the mists that surround parts of Asral and Lulrien. Someone give me a weapon."

A shrill cry went out, and more glowing eyes appeared in the distance.

"Too late," Ceara muttered. "Give me a weapon."

Ann tossed Ceara her knife then raised her hand, sending out a stream of fire. The first baneling blew up, but the others scattered and came at them from all directions.

Ed and Jax had gone off to find food and Sage had fallen asleep.

"Sciath a chosaint." Ann cast a protection spell around the sleeping druid.

Ceara hacked at the first beast who came at her.

Ann raised both her hands, sending out streams of fire.

"Urien must have sent them to track us," Ceara said.

Ann continued sending out fire in all directions. Blood pumped in her ears and adrenaline rushed through her. She spun and kicked another approaching baneling as it came at her, her long black cloak billowing around her.

One of the banelings knocked Ceara to the ground, snapping at the Gliss as she struggled to hold it back.

Ann grabbed her other knife and hurled it at the creature. The beast howled; Ceara shoved it away. "Blow it up."

Ann sent out another stream of fire. More beasts swarmed around them. Every time she took one down, two more seemed to appear. *Ed, where are you?* she called. *We need you.*

She didn't have time to wait for a reply and hurled another fireball at an oncoming baneling.

"There are too many of them!" Ceara yelled.

Sage scrambled up, raised her hands and caused vines to rise. Each vine turned and twisted, wrapping around the creatures like tight ropes.

One of the creatures was knocked down as she fired at the oncoming swarm.

Something flashed as it whizzed through the air, hitting the baneling. The creature disintegrated as the arrow passed through it.

More arrows hissed through the air. Each one flared with glowing light. The creatures fled as Ann hit them with another round of fire.

"Where did those arrows come from?" Ceara glanced around, searching.

Ann scrambled up and group of men emerged from the trees. They all wore grey cloaks and held bows.

"Druids."

Ann gasped as their leader walked over to her. "Jerome."

His lips curved into a smile. "Hello, Rhiannon. It's been a long time. Welcome back."

CHAPTER 8

"What are these bloody things?" Jax muttered as he swung his staff at a skeletal beast that came at him. Another one of the creatures bit him. Orange light flashed around Jax's body as he called on his strength to harden his skin. The baneling slashed at him, trying to dig its claws in. Jax caught hold of the creature by its front paws and tossed it away from him. Swinging his staff, he sliced its head off in one swift move.

"My guess would be banelings," Ed growled. The beast in him clawed to get out, wanting to rip the strange creatures apart. Again, he relied on his sword instead of his inner beast. He didn't want to risk losing control.

Ed, where are you? Ann called. *We need you.*

So much for that plan. Guess I will have to let the beast out. Ed's eyes flashed, his claws and fangs came out. He grabbed the nearest baneling and threw it against a tree so hard it exploded. His sword hissed as he shoved it back into its sheath.

"Ed, there are more of them!" Jax yelled.

He turned, spotting a horde of banelings coming toward them like an oncoming swarm. *Oh no, not more of them.* He needed to get to Ann, but that didn't look like it would happen. Not with these creatures around. No doubt Ann and the others would be surrounded by them, too.

Ed glanced over at Jax. "We need to get rid of these things as fast as possible. The others are in trouble."

Jax shook his head. "I think we need to worry about ourselves right now, brother."

"Damn, I think I would have preferred if they were Gliss." Ed's eyes flashed from amber to emerald as the first banelings leapt at him.

Ed knocked the first creature away and caught hold of the second one by its throat. His claws scraped against its bones. How such creatures were even alive puzzled him. He didn't have time to ponder the thought in the midst of battle.

In one swift move, he tore the creature's head off, tossing the skull away. The remaining body crumbled into dust.

"Jax, aim for their heads. Try slicing them off. It seems to be the quickest way to kill them." Ed called to him.

"I don't know if we can take all of them by ourselves," Jax called back.

Ed grabbed hold of another baneling. The tiny creature's teeth snapped at his fingers as he attempted to wrench its skull from the rest of its body. He winced as the teeth sliced through his flesh like tiny knives. More of the creatures surrounded his feet, nipping at his heels.

Jax swung his staff, orange light flashing around his skin as he protected himself and prevented the banelings from biting or scratching him. *Ed, we need to do something. I can't keep this up forever. It's hard to protect myself and use a weapon at the same time.*

More and more banelings bit him, their teeth and claws like a thousand needles against his flesh. His inner beast growled. Ed blurred, throwing all the creatures off him as he went. Damn, there had to be an easier way of killing them.

He moved over to his brother's side, shoving several of the banelings away as Jax doubled over gasping for breath, unable to harden his skin any longer.

Any ideas? Jax asked.

I'm thinking... Ed growled, his eyes flashing as more banelings advanced toward them.

Together they started taking down the banelings one by one. It took too long for Ed's liking. He bared his fangs, he roared so all the creatures scattered.

"Nice one, brother." Jax grinned, leaning on his staff for support. "You should do that more often. It could save us from a lot of future battles."

Ed blurred away before Jax could say anything else. *Ann, are you alright? I'm sorry I couldn't get to you sooner. We were surrounded.*

He stopped close to the stream and spotted Ann and Ceara with a group of five druids. He recognised one of the men talking to Ann. The man had short brown hair, a chiselled face, and deep blue eyes. Jerome.

What's he doing here? Ed's heart twisted at the sight of seeing Ann with one of her old lovers.

"Hey, wait for me." Jax puffed as he sprinted over. "It's not fair you being able to—hey, who's that? Druids? I thought we still had a few miles to go."

Ed stared at Ann smiling as she talked to Jerome. Something twisted inside his gut as the beast retreated without him even thinking about it.

"Who's that?" Jax repeated.

"Jerome Finn. He was Ann's boyfriend back before the revolution." He scowled. Seeing him with Ann again made him want to twist the man's head off. *By the spirits, what's wrong with me? I'm not the type of person to get jealous.*

"I remember him," Jax said and touched Ed's shoulder. "You should tell Ann how you feel before that guy sweeps in and steals your woman."

"She's not mine. She never has been," he muttered. "I can't be with her anyway." Not when he had this thing inside him that he couldn't understand, much less control. Why did Jax have to bring up his feelings for Ann now?

"Oh, for the love of the spirits, just tell her," Jax snapped. "You've been avoiding your feelings for over a decade. Time to admit the truth, brother."

Ed shook his head and headed over to the crowd. "Ann, are you alright?"

Ann's gaze shifted from Jerome to him. "Yeah, where were you?"

"We had a run-in with some nasty buggers," Jax answered. "They surrounded us. Sorry we couldn't get to you sooner."

Jerome's gaze flickered to Ed, too, and he frowned. Ed had never got along with the other druid and had never thought him good enough for Ann either. He'd been relieved when Ann had ended things. She had been with other men over the years, but none of them had been serious like Jerome. None of them had lasted long as he had—which had been several months. The longest Ann had ever spent with any man.

Why, of all people, did it have to be him? He would have preferred an attack by Gliss or even by Urien himself to this.

"We were attacked by banelings too," Ann said. "Urien must have sent them to track me."

"So why are you here?" Ed demanded of Jerome, crossing his arms.

Jerome didn't react to Ed's outward hostility. "We sensed the power of the archdruid." He smiled and kissed the back of Ann's hand. "I knew we would see each other again."

Ann blushed, and Ed felt about ready to kill the other man. Ann never blushed over anything. What was wrong with her? She never acted like this around men. She would've slapped any other man who dared touch her like that.

"It's good to see you." Ann smiled. "It's been a long time. We'd be happy to have you escort us to Trewa."

"We should get moving," Ceara said. "The banelings could still come back. I'd rather not have to fight more of them of today." Ed noticed the Gliss had dark circles under her eyes, and her usually pale skin looked almost translucent.

"Ceara, are you alright?" Ed asked in a low voice.

Ceara arched an eyebrow at him. "I'm surprised you'd care, wolfy."

"I still don't trust you," he lowered his voice so the other druids wouldn't hear him. "If you're going to drop dead on us, I'd like to know beforehand."

Ceara's eyes narrowed and she scowled at him. "I'm fine. No need to fuss over me. I'm not going to drop dead on anyone."

"We'd be honoured to escort you to Trewa," Jerome said to Ann.

"Ah, thank the spirits. I'm weary of all this travelling." Sage sighed with relief.

Jerome glanced at Ceara, frowning. "You can't bring the Gliss there, though. Is she a prisoner?"

"Do I look like a prisoner?" Ceara crossed her arms and raised her chin.

"She's coming with us," Ann said. "She's one of my rogues."

Ed's eyes widened. Rogues was a term for Magickind who didn't have any affiliation or loyalty to the other races. They were outcasts, unwanted by others. Ceara was a rogue herself, after betraying Urien and her fellow Gliss, but that didn't make her one of *Ann's* rogues. She still couldn't be trusted.

Jerome had a point. But Ann wouldn't be swayed on the matter, and he'd given up trying to convince her otherwise. She had to see Ceara's true nature for herself.

Still, Ed was surprised when Ann told him how Ceara helped her fight off the banelings. He'd expected Ceara to have run off by now. What was she up to? The Gliss must be after something; he just hadn't figured out what yet. Or else she would have gone running back to Urien by now.

The druids walked ahead, whilst Ann, Ed, and the others followed on horseback. The grasslands gave way to dense forests. The air filled with the smell of earth, leaves and pinecones as they moved deeper into the trees.

"I told you the druids wouldn't be very welcoming toward a Gliss," Sage said to Ann. "You can't afford to have them turn against you."

"I trust her. She hasn't done anything wrong," Ann hissed. "You shouldn't judge someone just because you think she's evil."

"Gliss aren't *good*, are they?" Sage snapped. "You're the archdruid. You need to start acting like it."

Ed had to silently agree, and Sage gave him a look. *Talk to her. She listens to you,* she said.

Sure, she does. When she feels like it. Ed bit back a laugh.

"Ann, she's right. We need the druids on our side or Urien may—

" Ed said to her instead.

"Ceara stays and that's final." Ann raised her chin and urged her horse ahead of them.

"She has Darius's stubbornness," Sage muttered.

Ceara moved on ahead, following close behind Ann. Ed scowled at that. *His* place was by her side. Ceara had never joined the Black.

"Did she do anything to hurt Ann during that baneling attack?" Ed asked.

Sage shook her head. "No, but that doesn't mean she won't turn on us. She's done it before. I remember when she was a teenager. Ceara was besotted with Urien even then. She wouldn't have turned against him."

"Don't be so sure. Nothing like a woman scorned," Jax remarked.

The great standing stones marked the entrance to Trewa. The ancient stones stood in a great double circle. From the bluestones to the great sarsen stones that formed the outer circle. The stones stood like silent sentinels, grey and weathered from standing for many millennia. Ed always wondered what they would have looked like in the early days. Ann had created a spell once to show him, it had shown a double ring of stones. No one really knew what they had been meant for. Some of the earliest history in the five lands held theories on what they had been meant for. The druids had been using them for as long as anyone could remember.

Ed felt the crackle of power against his skin. Energy radiated from the ancient circle. Once they had been a monument for ancient man. Now they protected the way to the town.

Ahead, houses sat gathered beneath the trees. Each house was made from wood, mud bricks, and had a thatched roof and shuttered windows. Some of the walls had even been painted to make them look more attractive. It looked just as Ed remembered when staying here as a child. Flo and Sage had often travelled here for Sage's role as an adviser to the archdruid.

Children and animals ran around, whilst other people moved about carrying firewood or digging earth. Woodsmoke billowed out from the houses and the sweet scent of broth filled the air, reminding him of home.

All eyes turned to them as people stopped what they were doing and threw curious glances their way.

Ed urged his stallion forward so he, not Ceara, rode alongside Ann. Just as he always had when she'd been the archdruid's daughter and he one of the Black. Jax came up on Ann's other side. It almost felt like the old days as knights of the Black Guard. Except now, Ann, not Darius, came to Trewa as the archdruid.

The archdruid had once been the ruler of all the five lands. An avatar to the gods themselves in the days of old. Darius' position had given him a very different role. He'd been a monarch in his own right in Caselhelm and ruled over the lands with an iron fist. He'd worked with the council of elders to create laws and try to bring peace to the lands for the first time in centuries.

Ann still had his title and his power, yet as an outcast, she had none of the lands, armies, or responsibilities that her father had had.

Ed heard Ann's heartbeat quicken. He guessed she'd be nervous.

Just be yourself, he told her.

She gave him a grateful smile then shook her head. *I'm not ready for this.*

I doubt your father was either the first time he came here as the archdruid. He reached over and squeezed her hand. Jerome glanced back at them, frowning.

I doubt my father was ever afraid of anything. Ann laughed.

They rode past the standing stones, and Ed felt static charge against his skin. His inner beast recoiled at the sensation. *Too bad,* he thought. *The druids are my family too. At least Flo and Sage are.*

The druids might be one of the most tolerant races, but he didn't know how they would react to him now. He wouldn't be surprised if they cast him out or refused him entry as they had tried to do with Ceara. After all, they might consider him a danger to them.

Not pack, a low, guttural voice replied.

His eyes widened in shock. Could the beast talk now? That had been unexpected. Ed didn't know what it meant either. The thought disturbed him. He couldn't afford to worry about this.

People came running out of their houses, and more appeared as a crowd formed to stare at them. The sight of so many people made him uneasy. They didn't appear threatening, but they set his beast on edge.

Stay calm, he told himself. *They're not threatening you. I won't lose control again.*

"Have they come to gawp or declare war on us?" Ceara remarked, rubbing the back of her neck. He'd seen her doing that earlier. Were her wounds recovering already?

"They haven't seen an archdruid in years," Sage said. "People will be curious."

Jerome and even more warriors came and surrounded them. A blond-haired man stepped forward. "No Gliss are permitted here," he said. "We'll take this woman into custody and—"

Here we go. Ed's hand went to his sword. *Spirits, am I really considering defending her of all people? She's still our enemy.*

Jax, be ready, he told his brother. *I have a feeling this won't end well.*

Ann jumped down from her horse, pushing back her hood, her long leather cloak billowing behind her. "I'm Rhiannon Valeran…the archdruid," she said. "This Gliss is my friend, and will not be harmed by anyone here, are we clear? She's not a threat."

"She's a Gliss. She has killed—" the other man protested.

The hands of the other warriors went to their weapons as they prepared to fight. Ed jumped down from his own horse and drew his sword, the blade glittering in the sunlight. The hilt still had the emblem of the Black on it. Jax did the same and drew his fighting staff.

Ann crossed her arms. "She serves me. If anyone tries to harm her, they will suffer my wrath."

"With all due respect, my lady, you can't ask us to allow an enemy to stay here."

Ann's eyes flashed with light. The air crackled with electricity as the stones glowed with lightning. A true sign of the archdruid's power. Ed bit back a smile.

The men backed away. Someone clapped, and they all turned to stare at a dark-haired man dressed in long blue druid robes. Blaise Valeran. "The Gliss can stay," he said, then stormed off without saying another word.

CHAPTER 9

Well, that went even worse than I expected, Ann thought. But she'd be damned if she let anyone hurt Ceara. By the spirits, why did Blaise have to appear and disappear like that? The Gliss hadn't done anything to them.

"So much for good terms," Sage muttered. "Ann, I told you—"

Ann held up her hand. "Not now, Sage."

Ed and Jax both lowered their weapons. The druid warriors dispersed and moved out of their way.

"Phew," Jax breathed. "I'm glad we don't have another battle on our hands."

Ann told Jax to make sure no one harmed Ceara. She hurried after her uncle with Ed trailing behind her. He seemed to have slipped back into his role as one of the Black.

Blaise's own house was a whitewashed thatched cottage that appeared larger than some of the other buildings around it. To her relief, Jerome didn't try to follow them. Good; she would talk to him more later.

Why did Blaise have to clap his hands and make a scene like that? Sure, he might allow Ceara to stay, but he'd undermined her in front of the other druids.

Blaise looked more or less as she remembered. Where Darius had been golden blond, Blaise had dark blond hair, but he still had the same clear blue eyes as his brother. Wrinkles lined the corners of his eyes. His hands were worn and calloused from years of working with herbs and plants.

"Is that it?" Ann demanded as she followed her uncle into his house. "Is that all you have to say to me after all these years?" To her surprise, Ed stayed outside. She didn't know whether to be relieved or disappointed by that.

She moved through the hallway, stopping in a larger room. Herbs hung from the rafters. A couple of chairs surrounded the stone fireplace. A rug made from reeds covered the flagstone floor and the heady scent of incense filled the air. The walls were grey stone, not whitewashed like the outside. Shelves lined one side of the room, filled with jars, coloured bottles, and small vials. It looked just as she remembered. Blaise always had kept everything neat and organised in his own particular order.

Blaise glared at her. "I've kept these people safe for years, and you come waltzing in like you're the archdruid."

"I am," Ann said through gritted teeth. She might not like the title or rank—a lot of good it did her—but she couldn't deny she had the power.

"That doesn't mean everyone here will just fall in line to follow you," Blaise said. "The world has changed since your father's reign. How dare you storm into my town and threaten my men, all to protect a damned Gliss, no less!" He clapped again. "Bravo, niece. You certainly inherited your father's arrogance."

"Your men threatened one of my people. You can't expect me to stand back when Ceara hasn't done anything wrong." She should've known Blaise wouldn't give her a warm welcome, yet part of her had hoped her father's death would've changed things between them. Wasn't death supposed to bring people closer together?

"The Gliss killed more than a dozen of my best warriors last month. They've spent the past few years hunting our people to extinction," Blaise said, his jaw tightening. "Yet you protect one of them. You can't expect me to welcome her. They're our enemy. Orla declared war on us after your father's death. It's her mission to wipe out the entire druid race."

Ann crossed her arms. "I didn't come here to argue about a Gliss. I came to—"

"Oh, I know why you've come. I know that bastard brother of yours is back, ready to plunge the lands into chaos," he said, moving around the table and picking up a pestle and mortar. "After all the years you spent in hiding whilst our people and the rest of the lands suffered, you—"

"Urien killed my parents and Orla's forces brought about the revolution. I stayed in hiding to make sure Orla didn't get Urien back," she snapped. "If I'd come here, I would have put everyone in even more danger. I stayed away to keep you and the other druids safe."

"Yes, now you come grovelling to me. But you'll find no allies here, niece. It was Darius' ambition that brought about the revolution," he said, his eyes hard. "I won't have you drag these people into another war. It would be better if you all died that night, and the Valeran name died with you."

Ann couldn't believe it, and her mouth fell open. She hadn't expected this much hostility. "I didn't come here to beg for your help. I came because I thought it was time we mended the rift in our family," she said. "You want to protect your people, I respect that. I'm not here to undermine your leadership."

Blaise laughed. "No, you've made it clear why you came. You need something from me—the support of the other druids," he said. "That's what your father used people for, too. He got what he needed, then he cast them aside once they served their purpose." His grip tightened on the pestle and mortar so much his knuckles turned white. "You're even worse than he was."

"You don't know anything about him!" Ann cried. "He wasn't perfect, but he was still my father, so don't speak ill of him."

"Get out. You may be the archdruid, but I don't want you here. Stay if you must; I don't have the authority to cast you out," he said.

"And I don't have to be welcoming."

Her fists clenched. "You haven't changed either. You may hate Papa, but you are more like him than you think," she spat. "I only came to warn you of Urien's return—that's done now."

"You came because you need allies."

"I don't need anything from you," she hissed. "I've been alone since the night I found my mother dead and watched Urien kill my father, who died in my arms. Part of me died that night, too. I'd be dead now if Papa hadn't cast a spell. I spent the last five years trying to make sure Urien never came back. Now he's inside the body of my other brother, and I don't know how to save him." Hot tears filled her eyes. "You're lucky to have people here to help you. Xander and I fought Orla's forces with only Ed by our side. You're wrong, uncle. I don't want anything from you." She stormed off, horrified she'd started crying. Blaise was one of the few family members she had left. Ann had hoped he might have been a little more welcoming. She hadn't meant to offend him, but she couldn't let anyone hurt Ceara.

Ann had thought about staying here among the druids before now and had wanted to go to them after her parents died. But it hadn't been an option. She hadn't wanted to put their lives at risk, too.

She wiped her eyes with the back of her sleeve and pulled up her hood. "We are leaving," she told Edward, who had been waiting for her outside. "Ask if they'll give us new horses. Our old ones will be too tired to make another journey already." She stormed off, wanting to get away from everyone.

Some archdruid I am. Even my own uncle wants nothing to do with me. Part of her had felt like she was coming home when she'd seen the great stones again. It had reminded Ann of happier times, when she'd come here alongside Darius. He'd been feared and respected by their people. Ann didn't want any of it. Fire flared in her hand; she wanted to hurl it at something. Watch it burn and smoulder.

She moved out of the town through the tree line until she found the small secluded grove where Darius used to bring her.

Ann stopped by the old oak tree where they had left offerings to their ancestors. *You were wrong, Papa. I'm no archdruid.*

She didn't hear him, but she felt Ed's presence behind her. "I want to be alone," she muttered. "Go tell the others we're leaving."

"I've never seen you admit defeat so easily. Even when we were kids, you never gave up, Rhiannon."

Her eyes flashed as she spun around to glare at him. "I told you not call me that anymore."

"Ann, I know you like to think the old you is dead and gone, but we both know she's still in there," Ed said. "You proved that with the way you stood up for Ceara. You're not going to just walk away because Blaise doesn't want you here."

"I don't want to be the archdruid. I only came here to find a way to save Xander." Her hands tightened into fists. "What good would have having allies do anyway? I'm not going to war against Urien. I just want to save my brother."

"We've been on our own a long time now. I know you liked life the way it was when it was just us and Xander fighting the good fight." He put his hands on her shoulders. "I don't want this beast inside me any more than you want to be the archdruid. But neither of us can change what we are." He squeezed her arms. "Cry and scream if you want to, but the Rhiannon I know wouldn't run away when she knew we needed to be here."

Ann pulled away from him. "Don't you want to go back to being the way we were? Rogues, fighting the good fight?"

"We're still rogues, and we can fight the good fight," he said. "You know I'll always be by your side no matter what. Always and forever, remember?" Ed turned and walked away.

Ann slumped back against the oak tree, closing her eyes, letting her mind drift.

Darius stood beside her. Tall, dark, imposing. A giant of a man. It made her heart ache seeing the memory of him. *Papa, why can't you still be here? You were always meant to lead these people. Not me.*

She let the memory unfold before her. Let it take her back to a happier time.

"It's not working." She raised her hand, trying to make the leaves of the tree blossom by using her magic.

"You're trying too hard." He raised his own hand, making flowers spring up around her.

"I'll never be as good as you." She sighed. "I'm not that powerful."

"You already have power, Rhiannon. You're the strongest of all my children," he said. "Being a druid isn't about power. It's about strength and skill. Nature provides us with all the power we need.

The rest has to come from us. Our will, our determination. If you believe you can do anything, you can. Try again."

Ann took a deep breath and raised her hand. This time the entire tree became covered in bright green leaves.

Darius laughed. "There, you see? Remember that whenever you have a problem you think you can't solve."

Ann opened her eyes, letting the memory fade. Raising her hand, her fingers flared with light. All around her trees became covered with leaves and flowers sprang up, filling the air with their heady scent.

She rose and drew back her hood. She marched back into Blaise's house and took a deep breath. "I'm sorry if I offended you earlier. But understand I didn't come here to challenge you," she said. "Like it or not, I'm staying. I won't stand on the sidelines anymore. I tried to keep Urien away, to weaken Orla. That didn't work, but I won't stop until I save Xander and find a way to stop Urien for good." She stared at him. "We don't have to get along. These are still your people, not mine." She tucked a lock of hair behind her ear. "Maybe I can help while I'm here."

Blaise laughed. "Help with what? As you can see, we're managing just fine here. We have the stones to keep out the worst evils. Erthea provides all we need. Why would we need your help?" he retorted. "Last I heard, you and your rogues are wanted fugitives in all five lands."

Her lip curled. "You don't believe I killed my parents, do you?"

"It doesn't matter what I believe. I still don't want you or your rogues here."

Ann repressed a sigh. How else could she get through to him?

"The stones are weakening," she said instead. "Their power protects the druids when they're within its border. But that's getting less and less every year, isn't it?"

Her uncle's eyes narrowed. "What would you know about that? You're wrong. The stones have been around since the times of ancient man. They'll be here long after we're all dust."

"I can feel it, and I think you can too. While I'm here, I can—"

"No." Blaise slammed down his fist so hard the table shook. "I won't have you using the power of the stones for your own gain. Blessed spirits, you're no different from Darius. He used the stones—"

"Like it or not, I'm the only one who can use their power. The stones are tuned to the power of the archdruid. I'll do what I can to help keep you and the others safe."

Blaise's mouth opened and closed several times, but no words came out.

She turned to go. "I'm sure you can tolerate me for a few days." She glanced at Ed as he came inside. "We're staying."

"First a Gliss, now a lykae. You're asking a lot of me, niece," Blaise grumbled. "Do you control him, too? Then again, he always did act like your lapdog."

Ann frowned. "What's a lykae?" Her lips thinned. "And he isn't my lapdog. He's my partner, so treat him with some respect."

Her uncle snorted. "You don't even know what he is, do you?

He's more dangerous than a Gliss. Maybe even more dangerous than Urien."

CHAPTER 10

Lykae. Ed let the word roll inside his mind. It sounded somehow familiar, but he had no idea where he'd heard it before. Lykae—did he finally have a name for the beast? If so, where did lykaes even come from? Were there more out there?

Blaise's words: "He's more dangerous than a Gliss. Maybe even more dangerous than Urien" hit him like a ton of bricks. What could that mean? He'd never hurt Ann, Jax, or Sage.

"He isn't a threat either," Ann snapped. "Are you going to condemn every one of my friends?"

"Ann, don't," he said and turned to Blaise. "Do you know what I am? Why I have a beast inside me?"

"You don't *have* a beast—you *are* a beast, boy." Blaise laughed. "I didn't think you knew. I always wondered when you'd change."

Ed froze for a moment. Orla hadn't cursed him; the beast was part of him. He hadn't wanted to consider that possibility before now. He'd been in denial for weeks. Even though the others had suggested the beast might be a natural part of him, he never wanted to believe it.

"What is a lykae?" Ann asked. "I studied most of the races throughout the five lands whilst I was growing up. I've never heard of them."

"A creature that comes from one of the other lands. Maybe part of Asral that was lost to the mists, or Lulrien—most of that land vanished. They are a thing of nightmares." He glared at her. "If anyone here gets hurt because of your beast or your Gliss, I will hold you responsible."

"They won't," she insisted and took Ed's arm. "Come on, we need to check on the others." She tugged at him outside the door.

Ed sighed but pulled away from her. "See you in a minute." He headed back inside. Blaise might be one of the few people who knew what he was and how to control it. He had to find out what the druid knew about his lykae nature.

"If you want more answers about the lykae, I can't help you," Blaise snapped. "I only know what you are because Darius told me. He didn't elaborate on what it means, or how to help you. I'm guessing that's why he chose you to keep his daughter safe above all of the other Black."

Ed's eyes widened. Darius had known? He shouldn't be surprised by that. That man had a lot of secrets. Darius had even known he would die. He'd given Ed plans to help get Ann and Xander out of the palace and take them somewhere safe.

"What else did he tell you?" Ed asked. "Please, I need to know. You don't have to trust me, but I know you're a good leader and a good man. Isn't helping others what the druids used to be about?"

Blaze laughed again, this time without humour. "What does it matter? The druids are a dying race. As for what you are, no, Darius didn't tell me anything else." His lips curved into a dark smile. "Are you sure you want to know what you are?"

Ed hissed out a breath. "I don't have a choice in the matter. I need to know how to control it."

"I'm sorry; I can't help you. The lykae could come from beyond the mists. Given how you were in the sea when Ann found you, you could have come from anywhere."

Ed nodded, accepting defeat, then paused. "I thought you should know, Flora…" Just thinking of his foster mother brought to his lump to his throat. Ann didn't mention her aunt much, but then, she was good at blocking out her feelings. She always had been.

"Is gone now too. Yes, I know. I felt it. Both my siblings are dead. Darius was no surprise, but I never wanted my sweet sister caught up in this mess." Blaise continued pounding away at an herb mixture with his pestle and mortar. "I warned her to get away from all that. But no, she insisted on working with Sage and the resistance."

"Flora believed in working for better future, just like Ann does. Ann isn't Darius. You're on the same side, and you need to learn to work together," he said. "She can be a great leader, but she needs people on her side if we're going to stop Urien."

"You saw what my brother's lust for women and ambition for power cost the five lands." Blaise stopped pounding for a moment.

"We can't change the past, only work for a better future."

Blaise laughed. "Careful, you almost sound like a leader. You shouldn't be led by blind loyalty or the feelings you have for my niece."

"I don't stay out of out of loyalty. I know what she is capable of."

"Is it because you love her?" The old druid raised a brow.

Ed turned and left, letting Blaise's words settle over him.

Jerome led Ann and the others to where they could sleep during their stay in Trewa. Ed trailed behind, mind still reeling from everything Blaise had said to him.

He took them to a set of small wooden cabins close to the forest. They looked like they hadn't been used in years. Trees and heavy foliage had grown over them.

"This is the best they could offer the archdruid to stay in?" Ceara scoffed. "I think we would be more comfortable sleeping outside in the forest. Your uncle really doesn't want us here."

Ed opened a door to one of the cabins and it fell off its hinges. He raised a brow at Jerome, who flinched.

"I'm sorry we don't have better accommodation," Jerome said to Ann. "These cabins were used when we had more warriors here. We just use them for when we have refugees passing through from the other lands. Sage sends people here when the resistance needs places for them to stay."

Ann's eyes widened. "And here I thought my uncle wasn't interested in helping the resistance," she remarked. "Don't worry, Jerome. These will do fine. We'll only be here for a few days at most. We can make do."

Jerome nodded, then made his excuses and left them alone, much to Ed's relief.

"You can't expect us to sleep here, can you?" Ceara crossed her arms and started rubbing the back of her neck again.

"We can make do. We're rogues. We don't expect to stay in luxury wherever we go. Ann and I have slept in worse places than this before," Ed insisted. "Why do you keep touching the back of your neck?"

"No reason," she growled through gritted teeth. "When I agreed to join you lot, I didn't expect to have to sleep in a hovel."

Jax sniggered. "Don't worry, I'm sure you can enjoy your nice cosy bed when you go running back to Urien."

Ann scowled as she appeared inside one of the cabins. "This is my uncle's way of making sure we don't stay long."

"It's probably to keep the threat of a Gliss as far away from the other druids as possible," Jax remarked. "You can't blame him for that."

"How come Sage gets to stay in the village with the other druids?" Ceara grumbled.

"Because she's the only one of us my uncle likes," Ann replied. "After a bit of cleaning up, I'm sure we can make these places habitable." She raised her hand. *"Glan agus deisiú."*

Ed felt magic crackle through the air. Orbs of light sparkled around the two different cabins. The dust and debris inside melted away, revealing makeshift beds, a small wooden table and a couple of chairs inside each. Jerome had said he would have some mattresses brought in for them too. The first cabin proved to be the largest, with two bedrooms.

Ceara smiled. "Nicely done, oh mighty archdruid. Now, the next question is who is sleeping where?"

"Who says you're getting your own room?" Jax scowled at her. "You are still—"

"I'm sure Ann and Ed will want to be alone. Unless she wants to be alone with her former lover, that is." Ceara chuckled.

Ed's jaw tightened. "Why would Ann and I need to be alone? Jax and I will take the second cabin."

"Good, I'm not staying near Jax. He snores louder than a drunken pig."

"I don't snore," Jax insisted.

"Yes, you do," the others said in unison, which made them all laugh.

Ceara stalked off to her room once Jerome and a couple of the men brought mattresses for them.

Sage seemed the most relaxed among the druids and got chatting with them.

Jax got talking to some of the other warriors, too. Ed felt a little out of place among them, and instead stayed close to Ann. The other druids seemed to keep their distance from her, and especially Ceara.

After a few days, some of the other druids started to be a little less wary of her and finally started talking to her.

Ed got talking to the men, too, and got on well with most of them. Blaise hadn't revealed his lykae nature to them, much to his relief.

He noticed Ann spending more time with Jerome, too. Ed tried not to let it get him, yet seeing them together made it harder to keep both the beast and his strange new rage under control.

Ed went for a run every morning and evening. He ran a few times around the entire town. That eased some of the tension.

But being near Ann seemed to calm him the most. He had no idea why she seemed to have such an effect on him.

The first rays of dawn broke over the horizon. Noticing a light on in her cabin, he headed toward it. Ed heard only one heartbeat inside, so knew Ann would be alone. He knocked, and she opened the door. "You're up early," she remarked.

"I don't need much sleep now," he told her. "Not since I turned into a beast." She opened the door further to let him in. "What are you doing up?"

She shrugged. "Don't you find it strange Urien hasn't come after me again yet?"

Ed nodded. "I guess, but we've only been here three days."

"Urien is an impatient person. Now he's back, he'll want the five lands to fall under his rule as soon as possible," she said. "He won't sit and wait for people to fall in line. Nor will he want me to start getting allies." She paused and motioned him over to a map that lay on the table. "I've been trying to figure out what he's planning. What his next move will be."

"What does Ceara say?"

"She said she heard something about Urien calling all the leaders of the five lands together. He must have planned something big."

Ed sat down on the bench beside her. "He's already sent banelings after us. Not sure how he managed that; they're supposed to live in Asral, and parts of that land are blocked off thanks to the toxic mists."

Asral lay between Caselhelm and Vala. Some parts of it were inaccessible due to heavy toxic mists that had been around since before the dark times when ancient man and most civilisations had been wiped out. Things did occasionally come through the mists—strange, deformed creatures like the banelings.

"Urien must have found a way to pierce the mists," Ann mused. "Damn it, I wish I could access my father's vault."

"What?" Ed didn't recall Darius ever having a vault. He seemed to keep all his knowledge locked away within his mind. Darius hadn't even written down the things he'd learnt, for fear it would be used against him.

"Papa had a vault where he kept everything he valued. Books, objects of power, weapons. He never showed it to anyone—not even me," she said. "But I know it existed. I saw him go in more than once. A door would appear, and he'd disappear through it. He only shared things with me that he wanted me to know. But we both know he had a lot of secrets and used magic way beyond anything a druid could do."

"True. Do you think Urien found it?"

"I think Papa would have sealed it from him. He didn't trust Urien either." She glanced at the map again. "I've been trying to think where Urien would hold this meeting. Some leaders would have to travel a long way."

"What about the vault? Have you tried using your powers to access it?"

"Tried, yes, but I'm still wary of using magic. I don't want to draw Urien's attention." She frowned at him. "You haven't tried accessing any more of your memories since we came here either."

"You've been busy." Ed knew it sounded like a lame excuse.

"I'm not too busy to help you. Come on, let's go try again among the stones. I have a new spell I want to try, and no one will disturb us at this hour."

"New spell? Should I be worried?" He grinned. "Just because I'm different now doesn't mean your spell won't go awry."

Ann gave him a playful shove. "I could make you look like a beast all the time if you're not careful."

Together they headed out to the standing stones. Ann muttered a protection spell and the stones flashed.

Ed sat down, unsure if he wanted to remember more. He might have a name to go with the beast, but part of him felt terrified of remembering what might have happened to him.

"Try to relax," Ann told him. "It will make things easier."

"Last time, I remembered myself almost drowning and someone chasing me. It's hard to imagine anything good coming from it." He shuddered at the memory.

"Aren't you the least bit curious to learn if you have a family or not?" She sat down beside him, laying her cloak out on the ground.

"I already have a family. You and Jax are my family. Just like the Black were."

"Yeah, but we're not blood related."

From what he'd seen of her family, Ed didn't know if he wanted to learn more about his own kin. What if they were beasts too? What would they be like?

"You're tensing up," Ann said as she sat in front of him. "Breathe. Maybe put your head in my lap. It will be easier if I touch you."

Ed lay back, resting his head against her. He tried to ignore the pleasure it gave him just being near her, which only made him tenser.

"Would you relax?" She placed her hands on the sides of his head.

I would if you didn't smell so damn enticing, he thought, hoping she didn't hear that.

Ed squeezed his eyes shut and tried to think of anything but her.

Ann chanted words of power and the spell suddenly dragged them both in. Mist clouded the stones around them.

"We're not on Trin." He observed the landscape inside his mind as he sat up.

"This is a safe place, too. Let's begin. Go back to the time before Trin; where are you?"

The stones around him blurred away until he stood surrounded by trees so tall, they seemed to reach the horizon. These were unlike anything he'd seen in Caselhelm, or even a couple of the other lands he visited. They were skinny with dark blue trunks and blue leaves. The air smelled sweet.

"I know this place," he said more to himself than her. "They feel so familiar, yet I don't remember ever being here." Ed reached out, felt the rugged bark. He ran, the trees blurring past him, yet all he saw were more trees. "Why aren't I seeing anything else?"

"Maybe you're trying too hard." Ann's presence felt comforting at the edge of his mind. "Let the memories come, don't try to force them."

The forest blurred until he found himself running as a boy. Something chased him, he could feel it. Light flashed, along with a snarl and a heavy breath on his neck, yet he saw nothing.

Ed knew he had to keep running. He stumbled, his feet ripped bloody from wearing no shoes. Rocks dug into the soles of his feet, but he didn't care. He had to flee.

But why? Ed wondered. *Why am I fleeing? What's chasing me?*

The images around him flickered. "You are trying too hard," she warned. "These things have been locked away deep inside you for a long time. You can't force your mind to reveal them all at once."

Why not? I need to know more about this beast. The trees came back into focus and he ran to the edge of the river. Its purple waves churned and hissed.

"You can't run from me, boy," the voice came again. "You'll never escape me."

Ed backed away, his heart hammering in his ears. He turned and jumped, letting the heavy current drag him away. Hours seemed to pass as he floated away.

"Enough." Ed pulled back, finding himself back among the standing stones. Mist floated around them, cool and damp against his skin. "Try again." He glanced up at Ann.

"You can't force the memories, remember?" she said. "It could—"

"Just do it. Please."

Ann sighed. "Is stubbornness a lykae trait?" she muttered, resting her hands on the sides of his head again.

He chuckled. "I must've learnt it from you."

Ann said the incantation again.

Ed reappeared inside the forest. This time surrounded by green trees. The air smelled of fresh grass and pinecones.

Darius stalked through the trees, glancing behind him several times, as if he were afraid of being followed.

"This doesn't feel like a forgotten memory," Ed remarked.

Ann appeared beside him. "I know this isn't your memory," she replied. "I think it's mine. I remember this."

"Why would I be witnessing your memory?"

She shook her head. "I have no idea. Let's see what happens."

Darius did another scan then muttered words of power.

"He's checking to see if anyone followed him," Ann said. "I was hidden behind the trees. He didn't sense me."

Darius raised his hand and a glowing doorway appeared. It creaked open and Darius vanished inside.

"Where did he go?" Ed asked.

"I don't know, but that's it. That's how I know the vault exists." She clapped her hands.

Ed opened his eyes and found himself back among the standing stones. He sat up, missing the feel of their closeness. Being with her inside his mind calmed the beast. More than that, the beast seemed content, even inside the cage of his mind.

Ann raised her hands and closed her eyes. Nothing happened. "Damn it, why won't the door appear?"

"It will when it's meant to." He took her hand and squeezed it.

"Sorry I dragged you into my memories. I know how much you want answers."

He sat up and brushed her hair off her face. "What are friends for? I'll share my memories with you, feel free to share whatever you want with me."

She gave a harsh laugh. "Trust me, there are things in my past you'd never want to see."

I share everything with you, he thought.

The word 'friends' tasted bitter on his tongue. She wasn't just a friend. The connection between them went way beyond that.

But you can never let her know that.

CHAPTER 11

Ed walked outside his cabin the next morning. The first splinters of dawn had just appeared over the horizon.

"Good, you're up," Jax said from behind him. "Time for training to begin."

Ed gaped. "What training?" He ran a hand through his long hair, which was still damp from where he'd bathed.

"Think we'll call it beast training. Let's go, brother." Jax slung an arm around his shoulders and led a bemused Ed out to an open area.

Ann already stood there, waiting for them.

"What's going on?" Ed asked her.

"We figured you need practice with your beast side," Jax answered. "So we're going to test you and see what your beast is really capable of."

"We figured you'd say no, so we decided to just do it," Ann explained.

Ed glanced between them. "Er…you'd be right." He shook his head. "You're both mad. I'm not doing this." He couldn't believe they'd even suggest such a thing. Were they insane?

"Ed, you want to control this, don't you?" Ann put her hands on her hips. "The best way to do that is practice."

"Yeah, summon the beast and see what triggers it," Jax agreed. "It took me hundreds of attempts to control both my shifting and my stone strength."

"We've conspired together for months now. Time we had some fun." Ann grinned.

Ed shook his head again. "This is stupid. Foolhardy, even. I might kill both of you."

"I can't die. Plus your beast seems more protective toward me than anyone else."

"Come on, brother. What do you have to lose?" Jax asked.

"Your lives, for one." His jaw tightened. "No, we're not doing this." He turned to leave.

Ann orbed in front of him in a flash of light. "I can make it an order if I have to."

His lips curved. "You wouldn't."

She arched a brow. "Wouldn't I? You know better than to challenge me, you big lug."

"I'll go first," Jax said, pulling out his sword. "We'll practice with blades, since you keep carrying yours around even though you don't need it anymore."

Ed's eyes widened when he recognised Jax's sword as the one he'd used back during their days in the Black.

Ed pulled out his own sword, the metal hissing as it came out of its sheath. "How is a sword gonna help control my beast?"

"Maybe it will remind you that you haven't lost yourself." Jax lunged at him.

Ed blocked him, parrying with his own blade. The sword felt like an extra limb, a familiar weight in his hand.

He moved, parrying each of Jax's lunges and blows. His feet moved in a familiar dance. Back during his time in the Black, he'd been one of the best swordsmen in the Guard. It came to him as easily as breathing.

"See, your usual nonsense." Jax grinned. "You're anticipating my moves and you're in control."

"I had to anticipate someone's moves long before I became a beast," Ed said. He became aware of someone behind him. Ceara, judging by her scent. He raised his arm, blocking her as she made a grab for him. Then he spun, catching her by the throat.

"See, you're not powerless," she choked out. "You…can let go now."

Ed's eyes flashed from gold to emerald. The beast clawed at the cage of his mind. It wanted out.

"Ed," Jax said. "Let her go. We asked her to sneak up on you. It's important to see how your beast reacts to certain situations."

A familiar rage began to heat his blood.

"Edward," Ann rushed over and touched his arm. "Let her go."

At once, the beast settled, and Ed released his grip. Ceara backed away, rubbing her throat. She gasped and took several rasping breaths.

"Okay, next time try something harder," Jax suggested.

Ed grunted in response. The joy he'd felt soon faded. "I don't think this is a good idea," he said to Ann.

"Nonsense, you're doing great." She flashed him a smile.

You don't understand. I almost lost control again, he hissed.

"But you didn't." Ann patted his shoulder then moved away.

"Stop talking to Ann in thought," Ceara chided. "We're your family. You can say whatever you need to around us."

Ed scoffed. "You're not—"

"We need to test how your beast reacts to magic," Jax said. "Gliss, you're up first."

"Gliss magic doesn't work on me," Ed pointed out. He felt weary of these tests already.

Ceara's lips twisted into a smile as she raised her hand. Light pulsed between her brows.

"This isn't a good idea." Ed glanced over as Jax backed away to join Ann. "You've seen how I react to Ceara."

"You learnt to control your emotions as one of the Black. You can do it again." Jax leaned back against the fence.

Ed looked to Ann, heart pounding in his ears.

She just nodded.

What if I hurt her? he said, giving Ann a pleading look.

Just try.

"Come on, wolfy. You know you're angry. Here's your chance to take it out on me." Ceara's grin widened.

The beast came to the surface again, eager and desperate to be free, like a rabid dog scraping the bars of a cage.

"Let it out. Don't resist it. The more you fight, the harder it is to rein in."

Ed scowled at her and let out a low growl. "You'd know, wouldn't you? You're the one who forced me turn into this thing." His fists clenched, his claws digging into his palms.

Spirits, he didn't want to give into this. Ed only let the beast out when he had to. Not voluntarily.

"Come on, wolfy. Still resisting," Ceara goaded. "What are you so afraid of? Me or yourself?"

Ed snarled; fangs bared. Blood pounded in his ears.

"That's better." Ceara beamed. "See, changing is easy once you learn to accept it."

I'll never accept you, he thought. *Traitor.*

Ed danced around Ceara, watching her every move as light pulsed through her forehead. *Come on, what are you waiting for? Give me a chance to rip you apart.*

An image flashed through his mind of him comforting Ceara the day Xander discovered her affair with Urien. He'd consoled her and tried to tell her she had to choose. Ceara had chosen wrong. She picked Urien and betrayed them all.

Other feelings washed over him, regret, sadness. He snarled, fighting off the feelings. *Is this your way of trying to convince me to trust you? Because it won't work.* Ed lunged at her.

Ceara's hand shot up, invisible waves of energy pulsing from her outstretched palm.

Ed grunted as the waves hit him like an oncoming storm. Anyone else would have been paralysed by the oncoming torrent of emotions being thrown at him. Ed brushed it off, making a grab for Ceara.

Ceara kept her hand raised, the flood of power still washing over him.

You really want to kill me, Ed? Ceara asked. *You were right. I made the wrong choice. You'll never know how sorry I am for that. I've changed.*

Ed drew back as Ceara lowered her hand. "No, I don't," he hissed. "But it'll take more than that to gain my trust again."

"What just happened?" Jax asked as Ceara turned and walked away. "Hey, Gliss, I thought you were helping?"

"She did." Ed sighed and leant back against the fence. "Are we done yet?"

"No, you aren't done with me and Ann yet. Our little sister was just a test run. Attack me."

Ed gaped at his brother. "Are you out of your feathered mind?"

"No, I've been wanting to see if you are stronger than me for months now. Time to test it." Light flashed over Jax's hand as he punched Ed in the face.

It felt like being hit by a hammer. Ed's head reeled back. He saw stars, and pain exploded inside his jaw. "Argh, what was that for?" He closed his mouth as blood dripped down his face. "What did you do that for?" The beast growled, and his eyes flashed.

It didn't help seeing the smug look on Jax's face. He grinned. "No reason. Now, what are you going to do about it?"

Ed blurred and lunged at Jax, who sidestepped him. This time rage heated his blood once more as the beast rose to the surface once again.

"Come on, brother. Attack me," Jax goaded. "Even the Gliss could put up a better fight than you."

"You're bloody mad," Ed growled.

Jax threw a punch. Ed caught hold of Jax's fist before the blow had a chance to connect.

Jax swung into a kick. Each and every time he tried Ed anticipated and blocked Jax's moves. "Not bad, brother. Up for some tracking now?"

Ed winced as he forced the beast back inside. A wave of fatigue washed over him. His teeth, fingers and head throbbed. "No, I'd say that was enough. I'm done."

"Come on. We went through way more intensive training than that when we trained for the Black."

"No, I'm—" He turned to look at Ann, to ask what else she had planned.

Ceara crept up behind her, a shock rod in her hand. She jabbed it into Ann's throat, making her cry out in pain.

Red flashed before Ed's vision as the beast burst out. He didn't even think; he moved fast. His claws and fangs came out as he blurred. Ed tore Ceara away from Ann so fast the Gliss dropped the rod before she had time to react.

Rage heated his blood, hot and fast. It beat at the air around him. He didn't want to kill this time; that wouldn't be enough. He wanted blood. His fangs ached to sink into Ceara's flesh. To rip her apart limb from limb.

Stop… Ed thought, but he couldn't form the words to produce a coherent sentence. The beast had full control of his body now. Ed was just an onlooker.

"Ed, stop." Ann scrambled up. "Let go of her."

Jax ran over to them. "Ed, this was my idea. I wanted to see if Ann being danger—"

Ed didn't listen. He gripped Ceara, lifting her off her feet like a ragdoll.

"Ed, put her down," Ann said.

"Ed." Jax gripped his arm. "It was a test. Ceara didn't —"

Ed used his other hand to punch Jax. His fist felt like it slammed into a brick wall, but the pain didn't bother him. He didn't even flinch.

"Edward, stop." Ann threw up her hands. A blast of magic hit him hard and fast, impacting the air around him. Ed staggered, and Ceara flew through the air. She landed a few feet away, gasping for breath.

Ed lunged for her again. This woman, this *traitor*, deserved to die. The beast didn't care about logical reason.

Jax stepped in front of him, his skin flaring with energy.

Ed thrashed against him. "Move," he growled in a low guttural voice.

"Edward." Ann gripped his arm. "Stop. Change back. Right now."

He raised his hand, but the beast stopped. No, he couldn't hurt her. He wouldn't.

The beast retreated once more.

Jax gasped as his magic faded. "Phew, you had me worried for a minute there," he breathed. "But it proves my point. You always change when Ann's close." He turned to Ann. "You must somehow calm him."

Ed turned and blurred away. His mind raced as trees rushed past him. He didn't have a destination in mind, just needed to get away.

Orbs of blue light flashed as Ann appeared in front of him. He skidded, trying to stop mid-blur. Instead, he collided with her, knocking them both to the ground.

"Ow." Ann groaned as his body slammed into hers.

"Sorry—what are you doing?"

"I felt your pain, so I came to see if you were alright."

He sighed. "No, I'm not."

"You aren't accepting the beast and changing."

"No, it's not that." Ed shook his head. "It's when I lose control. Rage takes over. I…I lose myself." He rolled away from her, lying back on the ground next to her. "Something else takes hold, and it's unnatural. Like fire in my veins."

"Why do you lose control when I'm in danger? You stayed focused with Jax, and even Ceara. What is so different with me?" Ann asked.

Ed looked away, heart twisting. "It's different with you," he murmured, more to himself than her.

"Why?" she asked again. "Is because your beast is so damn protective of me?"

"I'm not that protective…at least I never used to be." He sighed again. "I don't know why."

"Jax says it's because you love me."

Ed sat up and gaped at her. "What?" He rubbed the back of his neck. "I mean yeah…of course I do but—" Spirits, why did he get so tongue-tied around her? Why couldn't he admit his feelings?

"We've been best friends for a long time. You know I care about you more than anyone else. I suppose it's natural."

"Right, and I feel the same."

He considered blurring away.

"Well, today was a good start. Told you could control it." She gave him a quick hug.

Ed held her close, enjoying the warmth of her body. If he could have stayed there in her arms, he doubted the strange rage would ever bother him again.

Ed scanned the village. He caught the scent of different druids. Jax, with his familiar smell of evergreen. Ann's rose scent and another—Jerome.

He gritted his teeth. *Get a grip. You've seen her with other men before. Nothing's changed.*

But he didn't scent Ceara—the one person he was searching for. Where had that Gliss snuck off to now?

Ed sent his senses further, listening, smelling. Ceara, inside her room. The scent of magic—smoke and sweetness blended together.

I knew she would try something. Ed thought of calling Ann, but she was otherwise engaged.

Jax, Ceara is up to something. Can you come back me up? Ed asked.

I'm on my way, brother.

Ed blurred to the cabin. A rush of feathers caught his attention. The feathers swirled and twisted. "Hey, wait for me," Jax hissed.

Ed put a finger to his lips. *Shush. She might hear us.*

What's she doing in there?

I'm not sure, but I smell magic. Ed opened the front door with a creek.

Must be contacting Urien. Jax pulled out his staff.

"Don't," Ed hissed. *We don't know what she's doing yet.*

"Let's find out."

Jax pushed past him and stormed straight into Ceara's room. "Gliss, what are you doing now?"

Ceara jumped. She sat on the floor with two candles burning.

"Ceara, what are you doing?" Ed demanded.

Ceara shut up and glared at them. "Gods, why can't I ever be alone?" she snapped. "Without you two stalking after me?"

"Good thing we did, too." Jax grabbed a bowl off the floor, then frowned. "What are you burning in here? Are you—?"

Ed took the bowl from him, taking in the different herbs. "These are used for spirit magic."

Jax's dark eyes flashed. "You tried to summon Urien's spirit?"

Ceara gave him a shove. "You are such an idiot. I was doing a ritual for Mum."

Jax and Ed fell silent for a moment, both stunned.

"Why?" Jax demanded. "Since when—"

Ceara's eyes flashed, and she blinked back tears. Ed could see traces of moisture forming around her eyes.

"It's a druid ritual to remember her by. I never got to do it before. Never got the chance to say goodbye." She looked away. "Like it or not, she was my mother too."

"We're sorry, Ceara." Ed held at the bowl out to her. She snatched it away, clutching it to her chest.

"Get out, both of you." She pushed her hair off her face. "I'm not contacting Urien. Why would I? I want that bastard dead more than anyone."

Jax rubbed the back of his neck. "We're sorry," he added. "I didn't—"

"Why don't you start again?" Ed suggested to her. "We'll stay."

"Why?" Ceara's eyes narrowed. "To make sure I'm not contacting the enemy?"

"No. Because Flo wouldn't want us to be like this. She was a mother to all of us. Let's remember her together."

Jax nodded. "He's right. Mum wouldn't want us to fight. Cast the ritual."

Ceara glared daggers at them as she set the bowl back on the floor.

Ed and Jax both scrambled to sit on the floor beside her.

Ceara muttered the words in the druid tongue.

Strange, Ed used to think she had never paid attention to that kind of thing.

"We ask the spirits to remember our mother, Flora Valeran." Ceara said. "May her soul wander free in Summerland."

Ed and Jax echoed the sentiments. Ed hoped Flora did find in the eternal Summerland.

They fell silent for a moment.

Ceara rummaged under her bed. "Gods, I need a drink." She pulled out a bottle of wine.

Ed rolled his eyes. "I'm not gonna even ask where you got that."

She flashed Jax a smile. "I learnt from the best."

"Hey, I was a kid." Jax protested. "I had to steal in order to survive."

"You still stole stuff even as a teenager," Ed pointed out.

"Can't help if I'm good at it." Jax grinned.

Ceara opened the bottle and took a swig. "Argh, wine. I could use some good hard ale."

"Share and share alike, sister." Jax took the bottle from her and gulped down some of its contents.

"Mum won't be happy to know you stole that," Ed remarked.

"Hey, it won't be missed. You should check their stock room. They have as much wine here as Darius did back at the palace."

"Remember when Darius caught Jax stealing?" Ceara said.

Ed chuckled. "Yeah, never seen him so scared before."

"I'm sure Darius would have beaten him if Mum hadn't convinced him not to." Ceara took another swig of wine.

Jax shuddered. "It was only two bottles. And, as I recall, it was your idea, sister."

Ceara giggled. "Oh yeah, and you never did tell Mum." Her smile faded. "I still can't believe she's gone."

Ed grabbed the bottle and took a long drought. "I know. I miss her too."

Jax snatched the bottle from him. "Damn, that bastard Urien needs to die."

Ceara's fists clenched. "He will."

Ed leant back against the bed. "It's strange, but I doubt Mum would have wanted that. She always believed in forgiveness and seeing the good in everyone."

"I doubt Ann forgives him," Jax scoffed. "Urien's got to be stopped."

"I agree. Let's not think of Mum's death. Let's remember her life," Ed said.

The three of them sat talking and drinking for the next few hours. It reminded Ed family ties never really died.

CHAPTER 12

After a long day of more training and scouring through Blaise's extensive library, Ann and Ed walked through the town later that night. Most people had retreated to their houses or the main dining hall at the centre of the village. Lights flickered in the windows as they passed by the different houses. She heard the murmur of voices coming from the dining hall, where they had left Ceara and Jax drinking with the other warriors.

"I dreamt of Xander again," she admitted. "It's hard to sleep knowing he's trapped and being forced to watch Urien do unspeakable things." She sighed. "Part of me wishes we could just go back to the way we were. Just three of us." Having her best friend and her brother by her side had got her through the past five years after the revolution.

"I miss it, too, sometimes. But we're still partners," he said. "I'll always be there for you."

She shook her head. "Don't make promises you can't keep."

His eyes narrowed. "What does that mean? When have I have broken my promise?"

"I feel like you're going to leave me." She couldn't shake off the feeling either.

"Why would I?" Ed's mouth twisted into a frown. Ann shrugged. "Even if I did, I'd still be there whenever you needed me. Always and forever, remember?"

Ann smiled and hugged him. She spotted Jerome walk out of the hall and stare at them and felt Ed tense. "What's wrong?"

He glanced over at Jerome. "Be careful around him," he growled. "I don't trust him."

"You always were jealous of each other." Ann rolled her eyes. "I never understood it. Neither of you would have anything to be jealous of." She and Jerome had only been a couple for a few months, but it had been her longest relationship. Since becoming a fugitive, she hadn't had time for anything serious. Not that she wanted anything serious. Ann didn't believe in the romantic kind of love. That was a thing of fairy tales.

"He broke your heart."

"No, he didn't. Our relationship ran its course. I'm not interested in romance right now." Ann headed toward her cabin to see if Ceara had slept there. "Ceara?" she called.

Ed came up behind her. "I smell sickness."

Ann hurried over and opened the door to the second bedroom, flinging it open. Ceara lay on the floor, unconscious. "Ceara?" She knelt and felt for a pulse at the Gliss' throat. It felt weak and slow.

Ed came in and picked Ceara up, setting her back down on the bed.

"Go get my uncle," she told him.

"Will he help?" He stared at her, looking unconvinced.

"He's the strongest healer here. I'll pull rank on him and force him to do it if I have to. Go."

Ed blurred away, and Ann pulled out her knife, cutting away the leather of Ceara's bodysuit. A deep gash in her abdomen looked rank with infection.

"Bloody stubborn Gliss," she muttered. "Why didn't you tell me you needed help?" Ann didn't remember seeing any wounds like this a couple of days earlier when she had first examined Ceara.

Ann had seen Ceara wincing a few times, but the Gliss had insisted she was fine. She retreated to her own room and grabbed her pack, pulling out different healing supplies as she moved back to Ceara's side.

Ed reappeared and dragged Blaise, who still wore a night robe. "What's going on?" Blaise demanded.

"Uncle, I need your help. Ceara needs a real healer. You have to help her. Please," Ann begged.

Blaise wiped sleep from his eyes and glanced over at Ceara. "You can't be serious."

"Aren't druids taught to always help others?" she demanded. "She'll die if you don't help." Blaise turned to leave, but Ann rounded on him. "I've never asked you for anything. All I am asking you to do is help her," she snapped. "Haven't enough people died already?"

Blaise sighed. "You are to tell no one of this," he hissed. "Go get my healing kit from my house. But I make no promises."

Ann moved outside, letting Blaise work. Ed disappeared for a few moments and returned with Blaise's healing kit.

"I'm sure she'll be alright." Ed wrapped an arm around her shoulders. "It'll take more than an infection to bring her down."

Jax came in. "Hey, what's going on?"

"Ceara is sick—it's bad," Ed answered.

Jax stiffened. "Will she be alright?"

Ann shrugged and shook her head. They'd just got Ceara back into their lives. She didn't want to see her old friend die now. They had lost too many people already. This was Ceara's second chance at a better life.

"Rhiannon, can you come in here?" Blaise called to her.

Ann hurried back in. Blaise had rolled Ceara onto her side and cut away the rest of her clothing. "Look at this," her uncle said and motioned to the back of Ceara's neck. "She has been spelled. Looks like some tracking spell—not that I'm an expert."

Ann moved closer and saw the rune that glowed with the outline of a spell. She reached out and pressed her fingers against the back of Ceara's neck.

"Be careful," Blaise warned. "You have no idea what kind of magic Urien used on her when he held her prisoner."

She closed her eyes and sent her senses out. The rune glowed brighter in her mind's eye. It shimmered with dark, potent magic. A spell cast not only to trace Ceara's movements but to inflict her with illness.

"Damn you, Urien. I should have seen this before now." She gritted her teeth.

Blaise shook his head. "I doubt you would have been able to detect it. The spell has been woven into her skin. It wouldn't have shown up until Urien triggered it," he said. "I've seen this type of spell before. They used them in the great wars to track escaping prisoners. The spell not only traces them but punishes them for daring to escape."

"I should be able to remove it," Ann said.

Blaise's eyes widened. "Are you sure you can? That's dangerous magic. If you interfere, the spell could transfer onto you. It'll kill you as well as her."

"I'll be all right. Thanks to Papa's spell, I can't die. I need to break the spell if you have any chance of healing her."

Blaise moved back to the doorway. "Be careful."

She nodded and rolled up her sleeves as she took off her leather cloak. Ann closed her eyes, drawing her power to her. She'd need to burn the spell out of Ceara's skin to truly break it.

Ann pressed her fingers against the spell, feeling the dark magic in it simmering against her skin. *"Súile olc shábháil."* Power pulsed from her fingers into Ceara's skin. The rune blazed with fire as Urien's magic tried to resist her own.

Ann's eyes flashed with light as she forced her power into Ceara's body. She traced each separate tendril of the spell, forcing her fire through Ceara's system to obliterate any trace of it. Fire rushed forth like an oncoming flood, flushing away the dark magic as it went.

Ann drew back, feeling drained. She swayed on her feet a little and Blaise caught hold of her.

"Nicely done. It would have taken me hours to do complicated magic like that. But then, you always were the gifted one, weren't you?" He gave her a faint smile. "Wait outside. I'll do what I can from here, but I think you stopped the spell in time."

The three of them waited until Blaise finally emerged from the room. "She needs to rest, but I think she'll heal. She's young and strong."

"Thank you." Ann touched Blaise's shoulder.

Her uncle nodded.

Ann went in to check on Ceara, who opened her eyes.

"I had the strangest dream a druid was touching me, then I had fire running through my veins," Ceara muttered. "And not in a pleasurable way either."

"Next time you get hurt, tell someone," Ann said. "I'll make it an order if I have to."

"Thanks, Ann," Ceara said. "No one else would have done that for a Gliss."

"You're not just a Gliss." Ann smiled. "Rest. I'll come and check on you later."

"I'll stay and watch over her if you want," Jax offered. Ann arched a brow. "What?" Jax moved past her, sitting down in the chair.

Ann went to see Blaise. "Do you remember my father's vault?" she asked. "A secret place where he kept things he never wanted others to see."

Blaise frowned. "Darius had many secrets. I can't imagine him keeping them in a physical place. He would never risk anyone else finding them."

"I believe he had somewhere that existed outside time and place. I thought it might help—I'm working on a spell to free Xander," she said. "I ripped Urien's soul from his body the night he killed my parents. I'll find a way to do it again."

"How?" Blaise asked. "We're druids, our power comes from nature. We have little power over the spirit." He snorted. "That would never have been good enough for your father. He tapped into powers that went far beyond nature. Dark and unnatural things."

"On the way here, we were attacked by a group of sorcerers. I...I think I bound one of them. Like—"

"Like Darius could. Yes, I'm well aware of your father's abilities. He did so often like to prove how much better he was with magic than I." Blaise sighed. "I can't help you understand your powers more, but I will help you with the spell if I can."

Ann spent the day working with Blaise and the others as they tried to figure out what Urien's next move might be. Upon hearing the news of a potential Gliss attack, Ann, Ed, Jerome, and a group of druids went out to investigate. They all helped a group of druids escape and get back to Trewa. It felt good fighting side-by-side with her father's people again—now her people.

Jerome had asked her for a picnic that night.

Ceara had already got out of bed, annoyed they had gone off and fought without her. The warriors were all celebrating, so Ann decided to slip out meet Jerome. They were old friends after all.

She found him at the standing stones. He had a picnic basket and a blanket laid out. "I thought you said we were having a drink?" she remarked.

"We are." He held up a bottle of wine. "I thought it be good for us to celebrate today's victory."

"We saved a few people, but Urien is still out there. I'd hardly call it a victory."

"Any victory —big or small—should be celebrated." He patted the blanket.

She sat beside him and he poured them some wine. "So, what's the plan?" she asked. "Get me drunk then seduce me?"

Jerome laughed. "Am I that obvious?"

Her smile faded. "Jerome, I am—"

"You're with Edward, I should have guessed." He looked away. "I saw the way you embraced this morning."

"Ed and I are just friends."

Jerome's jealousy of her friendship with Ed had been one of the things that had ended their relationship in the first place.

"I hope you and I can still be friends," she added.

"Of course. I always knew we'd see each other again." Jerome paused. "I missed you, Rhiannon."

Ann winced. No one ever called her Rhiannon anymore. She hadn't wanted them to. Rhiannon had died along with her parents the night of the revolution.

"Ann," she corrected. "I've changed since we last knew each other. I'm different now."

"You still look as beautiful as ever." He bent to kiss her.

A shrill cry filled the air.

Ann bolted up. "Banelings." More screams rang out.

She raced back and saw a swarm of creatures racing through the town, knocking down anyone in their path. Ann threw a fireball at the first baneling, knocking it to the ground.

Jerome came up behind her. "How did they get through the stones?" She spotted a misty silhouette, and a skeletal face smiled back at her—Xander's face. "Urien!" Ann hissed and bolted after him, her long cloak billowing behind her.

Urien laughed and blurred away.

She hurled several fireballs at the banelings and hurried after Urien's disappearing form.

Ann sprinted past the houses and several fleeing people. No doubt the banelings were just a distraction. He'd come to torment her, to prove he could find her no matter where she went.

Ann stopped, breathing hard when she spotted Urien leaning against one of the stones. "Unlike you to hide, sister." Urien smirked.

It sickened her to see Xander's face staring back at her. "Oh, wait, you did that for the last five years."

"Not like you'd force people to join you, brother. Or are they supposed fall in line given how great and powerful you are?" she retorted.

Urien's jaw tightened. "You won't hurt me. You love your precious Xander too much."

She hurled a fireball at him. It shot straight through him, hitting the stone with a loud boom.

"Trewa will soon be mine. You can't protect the druids forever."

"What good will that do? You hate the druids. You despise the fact you even have druid blood," Ann sneered.

"Soon I'll be more powerful than anyone. It doesn't matter if you're the archdruid. All the races will fall in line soon enough."

"How? Going to kill everyone when you round up all the leaders in one place?" She smiled at the surprise on his face. "Yes, brother, I know about that. And I'll be there to make damn sure you don't slaughter dozens of innocent people."

Urien laughed. "You can't hurt me. You won't. The banelings are just the first wave. What's coming next will be much worse."

He laughed and vanished in a flash of light.

Ann hurried back toward the village. She saw Jerome and the other warriors fighting the banelings. A chill ran across her mind, something darker and more powerful stalked beyond the boundary of the stones.

Urien, what dark powers have you been conjuring this time? She followed the presence with her mind, but couldn't get a clear image of what it was. A cloud of darkness swept around the stones. The ancient guardians stood there, silent, but glowing with light.

A baneling flew at her, knocking her to the ground. Ann gritted her teeth and set it aflame. She hurried back toward the stones, searching for the presence she'd felt. *Come on, where are you? What are you?* Fire formed in her hand.

The stones were lit up like beacons, which meant they were keeping something out. Something far worse than banelings.

Urien? No, she'd feel if it were him. The presence felt stronger. Darker than him.

"I know you're here. So stop hiding in the shadows."

A voice, low and harsh, laughed. "I'm beyond your powers, little druid."

"What are you? Did my brother send you?"

"I'm beyond your brother, beyond even the power of the stones," it hissed.

A burst of light shot through the barrier of the stones. It hit Ann in the chest, slamming her against them. She saw a flash of red eyes before everything went black.

CHAPTER 13

Ed wondered how the heck banelings had managed to get past the stones as he snapped the neck of one of them.

Ceara sliced through another one.

"Who let you have a sword?" he asked her.

She rolled her eyes. "No one *lets* me do anything, wolfy. Where's Ann?"

Ed glanced around, wondering the same thing. He didn't sense her nearby and sniffed. The smell of death and burning filled the night air.

"Have you seen Ann?" Ceara called to Jax.

"She ran off earlier," he called back and inclined his head in the opposite direction.

The beast growled at the edge of Ed's mind, edgy and wanting to get out. *Something's wrong.*

Ed moved past the other warriors, knocking aside any remaining banelings who got in the way. The coppery scent of blood hit him, and his eyes flashed red. The beast burst from his mental cage. His fangs and claws came out as he blurred. Jerome knelt beside Ann where she lay near the stones. Blood seeped from her head and her cloak steamed from where something had struck her.

Jerome looked up and gasped. "Blessed spirits, what are you?"

Ed shoved the man aside, sending Jerome flying through the air. "Mine," the word came out low and guttural. The beast now had full control. Ed tried to force it back, but it wouldn't relinquish control. It whined as he gathered Ann up in his arms.

Jerome lay unconscious where he'd landed several feet away.

Neither Ed nor the beast could muster any concern for him. He only cared about Ann. Ed brushed her hair off her face and his hand came away bloody.

Two banelings stalked toward him. Letting go of Ann, he grabbed both beasts by their throats and snapped their necks one by one.

A voice laughed, and a shadow stalked outside the glowing stones. "You've grown up, boy."

Ed froze, he knew that voice. It sounded like same thing that chased him from the blue woods in his memory.

"You," the beast growled. "You hurt what's mine."

The voice laughed, harsh and cold. "I wonder who's more of a threat to her. You or I."

Ed blurred and threw himself at the glowing ward cast by the stones. He cried out as the energy sent lightning coursing through him.

The shadow laughed. "Even the stones reject you. You don't belong in these lands."

Ed thrashed. Both he and the beast wanted blood, wanted to tear that shadow creature apart. Yet the stones' power repelled him. Light flashed around the ancient sentinels as he made to go through the circle once more.

Ed snarled. That thing had hurt the woman he loved. In one swift move he burst through the glowing energy and charged at the shadow. Static burned against his skin, but he felt no pain.

The voice laughed, and the shadow blurred away.

Rage heated his blood. He wanted blood, craved it. Ed didn't even try to regain control. The anger felt too strong.

Where did it go? We have to find that thing. He sniffed the air, but found no scent, and growled.

Behind him, he sensed Ceara and Jax.

"We need to get her back to the village. She's hurt," said Jerome, who Ed guessed must've woken up again.

"What happened?" asked Ceara.

"Ed?" Jax called.

Ed spun around and blurred back. Jerome touched Ann again and Ed felt the beast rage.

Mine, the beast growled.

I've got to get control again. Instead, he flew at Jerome. He grabbed the druid, slashing at him with his claws. Jerome cried out and pulled out a knife, plunging it into Ed's shoulder. Ed felt the sting of metal as it bit through his flesh.

"Ed, stop!" Jax snapped, rushing over and trying to get in between them. "Jerome, leave him alone. He's not a threat." Jax's touched Ed's arm. "Ann needs a healer. You need to change back."

With a low growl, he shoved the druid aside, knocking Jerome to the ground. "Don't touch what is mine." His eyes flashed emerald as he scooped Ann up into his arms. "Mine," he growled.

"You need to go," Ceara said to Jerome. "You're making this worse. Go get those scratches cleaned up."

"What? Do you really think I'm going to leave her with that thing?" Jerome pointed at Ed. "He—"

"Ed won't hurt her. Trust us," Jax said. "Back off, mate. The beast is very protective of her. Coming in between them will only make it worse."

Ceara touched Jerome's arm, light flaring over her forehead as her magic passed through the air. "Ann will be safe with him. You need to trust us when we tell you he's not a threat or a danger to anyone. He only acts like this when Ann's in danger."

Jerome looked like he wanted to protest.

"Oh, and don't you dare try to get the others to attack Ed," Jax warned. "It will only cause more unnecessary deaths. You do not want to mess with the beast, believe me. Like we said, don't come in between him and Ann."

Jerome still didn't budge. "But she's hurt. How do I know he won't harm her?"

"Go, now," Ceara commanded, pulling out one of her shock rods. "Or I'll make you leave."

Jerome reluctantly stalked off.

"Come on, wolfy. Time to turn back," Ceara said, still gripping her shock rod.

"Where did you get that?" Jax demanded.

"Focus, bird boy," Ceara hissed. "We have to get him to change back. But he's going to be a lot more difficult whilst Ann's unconscious."

Jax rubbed the back of his neck. "Right. Ed, we've got to get Ann to a healer."

Ed turned and started to blur.

"Not that way," Jax said, touching Ed's arm. "You can't go back looking like that. People will think you're gonna attack them. Change back into your normal self."

Ed growled. He didn't give a damn what he looked like. Only Ann mattered. If she needed a healer, he'd get her one.

Ed blurred back through the village and into Blaise's house. Colours and a blur of faces rushed past. Blaise stood scrambling through a cupboard, pulling out different vials as he went. "Blessed spirits. What—?"

He set Ann down on the wooden divan. "Heal. Help," he said, voice still guttural.

Blaise walked over and examined Ann's head wound. "There are others far worse—"

"Heal her." He grabbed the man by the throat.

Jax and Ceara both came running in, breathing hard.

"I wouldn't argue with him if I were you," Jax gasped. "It won't end well. Help Ann, or at least wake her up. She's the only one who can get him to change back."

"But—" Blaise protested.

"Do you want him to turn his rage on the village?" Ceara demanded. "Just do it and be quick about it."

Blaise sighed and muttered, "Why did I agree to let you people stay here?" He moved over to Ann's side.

"Because she's the archdruid and we go where she goes," Ceara replied. "Hurry up."

Blaise touched Ann's forehead. "Why does the beast only seem to respond to her?"

"We're not sure. Probably because he's in love with her," Jax replied. "You've got wake her up fast. We don't know any other way of changing him back. If he thinks she's still in danger, there is no telling what he might do."

Ed felt his patience wearing thin. He wanted blood, yet the need to stay with Ann proved too strong to ignore. He couldn't leave her. The urge to stay, to make sure she was safe, felt stronger than any rage he might have felt.

"*Leigheas agus mend.*" Blaise muttered words of power. The blood receded around the wound.

Ann groaned and opened her eyes. "Ow, what are you doing, Uncle Blaise?"

"We have a problem." Blaise motioned to Ed. "He's not in control."

"Ann, I don't think he can turn back," Jax added. "We need you to talk to him. You are the only one who responds to. He's already attacked Jerome."

"What?" Ann still looked dazed, her eyes glassy with confusion. "Is Jerome alright?"

Ed let out a hiss at the mention of Jerome's name.

"He's fine. Just a few scratches," Ceara reassured her. "Probably better if you don't mention him. Seems the beast has a jealous streak."

"Edward, change back." Ann clutched her head.

He didn't want to change. He had to track down and find whoever had hurt her. Ed would find that shadow and…

Ann scrambled up and moved over to him, stumbling as she went. "Change back." She reached up to cup his face.

The beast retreated, his fangs and claws retracted. Ed caught hold of her as she swayed on her feet. "What are you doing?" he demanded. "You should be resting."

"He's right, Rhiannon. You should rest," Blaise ordered. "Now if you'll excuse me, I have other people to attend to. One of you should keep an eye on Rhiannon for the next few hours." Blaise then left.

Ceara grinned. "You look much better, wolfy." She glanced at Jax. "Why does the beast react that way?"

"That's obvious," Jax remarked. "It thinks Ann—"

"Why don't you two go and see if anyone needs help?" Ed suggested. He didn't want Ann to find out the beast thought of her as his.

"Yeah, we should check on Jerome. You hit him pretty hard, wolfy," Ceara said. Ed wanted to strangle her. "And you mangled up that pretty face of his, too."

Ann glanced between them and frowned. "Why would you hit Jerome?" she asked. "Are you sure he's alright?"

"He's fine," Ed insisted. "I lost control."

"Yeah, the beast didn't like Jerome touching you. Lykaes are very possessive of their women." Ceara smirked. "You did tell Jerome Ann was yours, remember? Growled it, actually. He wouldn't even let us near you."

"Let's go, sister." Jax grabbed Ceara's arm. "You can tell me how the heck you got your hands on that weapon you're not supposed to have." He led her outside.

"I'm a lot more resourceful than you think, bird boy." Ceara grinned.

"Listen, it's not what you think. You know the beast is—" Ed began.

Ann staggered when she made a move.

"You're supposed to be resting." Ed caught hold of her again. "Now's not the time to be stubborn."

"You don't understand. Something's outside the stones—a shadow thing tried to get through. It hit me with power." She rubbed her ribs.

"I know. I saw it, too. You heard what Blaise said. You might have a concussion."

"I'm fine." She pulled off her cloak then lifted her tunic. A black bruise now covered the side of her abdomen. Good thing her cloak was spelled to ward off magical attacks and had taken the brunt of the blow.

"Does it hurt? I'll get Blaise back here."

"I need to get back to the stones," she insisted.

"No, you need to lie down and rest. The shadow is gone; I saw it leave."

Ann pushed past him and stumbled toward the door.

"Ann, you might not be able to die, but you're not invincible." He caught hold of her waist to keep her upright.

"Fine, carry me then, just do that blurring thing so no one else sees." She wrapped her arms around his neck as he picked her up.

Ed blurred back to the stones that now stood dark and silent. "I doubt we'll find anything." He carried her past the stones to where he'd seen the shadow. To his relief, the stones didn't try to repel him this time.

"I saw Urien earlier, too. He taunted me. This was his way of telling me he can get to me no matter where I am." She sighed. "But that shadow felt…different. More powerful than anything I've felt before." She glanced around. "Put me down."

"You can barely stand." He didn't want to risk her making herself worse just because of her stubborn nature.

"Put me down." Ann gave him her "don't argue with me" look.

Ed put her down but kept an arm around her waist. He felt magic on the air. It bristled against his skin. "I couldn't tell where it was either," he said. "It didn't have a scent."

"You lost control again?" She looked at him.

"You know the beast in me is protective of you."

"Possessive too, huh?" Ann arched an eyebrow. "It thinks I'm yours."

Ed rubbed the back of his neck. "I shouldn't stay here. The beast is becoming more uncontrollable. I lose all control when it comes to you. I should leave." He didn't want to talk about how the beast felt toward her. It only proved to be too embarrassing. One of these days he knew he'd have to admit how he truly felt, but it wouldn't be today.

Her eyes widened. "No."

"Ann, you should have seen Jerome's face when he saw me tonight. I'm a danger to everyone here. You can't protect me from everyone. What if I killed someone? If you hadn't brought me out of it, I could have done more than scratched someone."

"But you didn't. Maybe the beast is reacting to your emotions. You can't leave, not until we recover more of your memories. Even then...I need you with me." She touched his cheek. "We can find a way to control this thing. With some more practise, we'll figure out a way to keep it under control."

He sighed and squeezed her hand. "I hope so."

CHAPTER 14

Urien growled in frustration as his latest spell failed to produce any results. "Why won't it work?" He gritted his teeth.

I don't know why you bother, Xander remarked. *You'll never find Papa's vault. He would have spelled it so you couldn't locate it.*

"I'm you now, remember?" Urien muttered. "He wouldn't have kept *you* out. You might be the worthless one, but he trusted you."

Xander laughed. *I'm not worthless. That's you, remember? You're the bastard.*

"Really? I'm on the verge of gaining control of all the lands—not just Caselhelm. What good have you done, brother?" Urien shook his head. Why was he wasting his time talking to Xander? He had work to do, and not just finding the vault.

Orla had taken over things whilst he focused on the most important task at hand: forming an alliance with the elders again.

Who are these elders you keep thinking about? Xander wanted to know.

"Nothing you need to know about." Gods below, he'd been doing everything he could to stop Xander from hearing his thoughts. If Xander managed to reach limbo again he might be able to warn Rhiannon about Urien's plans.

I need to find that vault. It's the only way, Urien thought.

I never saw Papa have a vault, Xander remarked.

Urien gripped the desk and grabbed a jug of ale. Alcohol seemed to be the only thing that allowed him to tune Xander out, but it also dulled his senses, which made it harder to perform any magic. He took a long swig, feeling the booze burn the back of his throat.

He muttered words of power in the druid tongue. "*Cabhair liom an méid atá á lorg agam.*" Power vibrated through the air. Urien glanced around, scanning each wall for any sign of a door. Something that might indicate the vault's location. He moved from each corner, seeing nothing. Urien moved to the back wall and pressed a panel. The wall slid aside, revealing another room beyond. Books, crystals, jars and other things lined one wall. A huge fourposter bed covered in heavy blue linens took up most of the space. It still smelled like Darius in here.

Urien wanted to tear this room apart, but he kept it the same. This place provided a refuge when he needed to get away from Orla and the others.

Too bad he couldn't find a refuge from Xander's incessant voice.

Darius had used this place to spend time with his many mistresses and other liaisons.

Urien moved around the room, checking each wall for a sign. If the vault was anywhere, it would be here. Only Darius could access it; even the servants hadn't been allowed in here.

Where is it? It must be here somewhere. Urien ran a hand over the wall, expecting to feel a trace of power.

Nothing.

He moved to the next wall, shoving books and other items aside as he ran his hand up and down. Still nothing.

Static flared between his fingers as he set the shelf aflame. The wood crumpled away into dust. He tore away the wallpaper. Why did Darius even have decorative paper on the walls? No one else in Caselhelm use this kind of decoration. Underneath, it revealed cold stone.

"Argh." He let out a cry of frustration.

What makes you think Papa hid the vault here? He wouldn't make it easy to find, Xander said. *Think of all the enemies he had. He wouldn't risk someone finding it out in the open like this.*

Urien opened his mouth to yell at him but stopped. "Hmm, you could be onto something there." A smile spread across his face. "I need to think more like the archdruid. Where would I hide something I didn't want to be found?"

His mind raced, and more of Xander's thoughts echoed as Xander tried to distract him.

Where would Darius hide things he never wanted to be found? Perhaps not here, but then where? One of his other residences? Urien remembered this being Darius's base of power. It was why Orla had taken control of the palace.

Urien grabbed another book, scanning the pages as if they held the answers he sought.

He tossed it aside in disgust. *Gods below, I need something to bargain with if I'm ever going to get them onside.*

Xander's voice faded into the background.

He needed the elders onside if he were ever to gain true power.

His mind drifted back to the time he was trapped on the other side. For five long years, his soul had been trapped in the nether realm. At times, he'd been able to glimpse things. There seemed to be few limitations in that land, but Ann's spell had kept him bound, unable to move or do anything.

"Death…that's it." He smirked.

On the other side, he'd be able to see. Maybe even spot the vault.

Urien pulled out his dagger. "Don't get too excited, brother. You'll still be bound." He plunged the blade through Xander's chest.

Urien almost shuddered as the mists of limbo surrounded him. Coldness crept into his very soul. This land wasn't meant for the living.

If Ann and Xander could wander around here, why couldn't he?

Urien made a move, but something held him in place. A tether to Xander's body.

Damn it, Ann moves around all the time! Why can't I? Still he remained rooted in place. Unable to go anywhere. He growled and muttered words of power.

Where is that vault?

Someone laughed, and a shadow darted through the mists. Urien scanned with his senses but couldn't detect what the presence was.

"Who are you?" he demanded.

Xander? No, he'd be trapped inside his body. Urien made sure of that.

The shadow darted back and forth, flickering in and out of the mist. "You Valerans like to wander in death, don't you?"

"Whoever you are, show yourself."

More laughter seemed to be coming from all directions.

Urien raised his hand. No power came to him.

How could that be? He'd seen Ann use power on this side of the veil. He held out his hand. Nothing, not even a flicker of magic came to him.

The shadow creature cackled. "You have no magic, do you?" it said. "You, like everyone, are powerless on the side of the veil."

"Rhiannon does," he hissed.

"You're not your sister. She's not a demon or mere druid."

He gritted his teeth. "Then what is she?" he muttered. "You still haven't told me who you are. Are you friend or foe?"

Another cackle. "Neither, but you want something, don't you?"

"Right, I want my father's vault."

The shadow moved closer, and Urien yelped as claws struck his skin.

"Argh, what did you do that for?" He clutched his shoulder. How could he be injured in spirit form?

"Because you lied," the voice growled.

"I didn't. I need that vault." He looked down, surprised to see drops of what looked like blood. Since when could spirits bleed?

"But it's not all you want, is it?"

"No, I—" Urien frowned. "How do you know what I want?"

"Remember, demon. Blood released you, blood binds you, and blood can bring you what you seek." The shadow darted away.

"Wait, come back. Tell me…"

Urien gasped, rasping for breath. His chest heaved.

"What's going on?" he asked. No, he hadn't spoken. Xander had. *Gods below, he's in control!*

Xander scrambled up, stumbling over the to the mirror. He reached up and touched his face. "I'm…I'm myself again."

No! Urien roared. *I own this body now, not you.*

Xander smiled and took a deep breath. "Now you know what it feels like. To shout and scream but be stuck inside where no one—" Xander doubled over coughing.

Urien took a deep breath and breathed a sigh of relief. "Little side-effect of crossing over. I won't let that happen again."

No! Xander screamed.

Urien moved out of the secret chamber, closing the wall behind him.

Outside his study, he called the guards to bring a servant in.

A young Ursaie walked in. Her horns peeked out through her hair and her bicoloured eyes shone with fear.

A demon slave. Even better, Urien thought.

What are you doing? Xander demanded.

The woman kept her eyes fixed to the floor. She wouldn't speak unless spoken to. Ursaie were considered inferior among Magickind. Little more than demons.

Urien knew the enslaved race still had ancient power in their veins. He ran a finger down her cheek. Funny, he'd always found the Ursaie strangely attractive. Too bad he wouldn't have a chance to take this one to his bed.

I won't let you rape this poor woman, Xander snapped. *Forcing a woman—*

I've never forced anyone. Urien pulled out his dagger, the blade still slick with his own blood. His sliced it across her throat.

The Ursaie's eyes widened in shock as she collapsed into his arms. Urien recited words of power to reveal what had been hidden.

Blood magic was always potent.

No! Xander yelled. *You—*

Urien stumbled as power washed over him. He caught a flash of the door, but the image faded before he had a chance to see where it was.

CHAPTER 15

Ann knelt outside the great stones the next morning as the first rays of dawn broke through on the horizon. Just as the night before, she found no trace of the strange presence. Damn it, all magical creatures left *some* trace behind. What was that thing and what did it want?

"So we're looking for a shadow?" Ed asked. "That's new."

"It's not just a shadow. It had power—enough power to knock me out and get through the stones." Ann ran a hand through her hair and glanced at Ed. "Did you notice anything else?"

He seemed quieter and more on edge than usual. "No." Ed shook his head. "It seemed to know me though." He paused. "I think it might be the thing we saw chasing me in my memories."

"What memories?" Jax asked as he came over. "From when you were imprisoned by Orla?"

"No, Ann has been trying to help me remember my life before I landed on Trin," Ed explained. "So I can maybe get some control over this damned beast."

"Ann already helps you to control it," Ceara pointed out, taking a gulp of her rakka tea.

Ed winced at the sharp aroma it gave out. "Do you have to drink that stuff? It's vile and it smells worse." He covered his nose, then shook his head again. "That's not enough. I need to know why I lose control and how I can control it."

"I think we all know that reason. Your beast told us last night." Ceara rolled her eyes and sipped more of her tea.

"That shadow thing felt different," Ann said. "Urien must somehow be trying to break through the mist into Asral or Lulrien."

"There are ways to break through the veil."

"Glimpsing the upper realm of Asral is one thing. But he seems to be bringing things through," Ann mused. "That's supposed to be impossible."

"Darius could have done it," Jax said. "Demons are supposed to come from beyond the mists. It's probably how he hooked up with Orla."

Ann winced. She hated thinking of Darius being with that demon bitch who'd helped kill both her parents.

"Maybe." She pulled up her hood. "I'm going to an old temple not far from here where I'll focus on finding some answers," she told them. "Ed will come with me. You two go scan the surrounding area. The other druids are checking if the stones' power has been breached. Go help. See if you can track where the banelings are coming from."

Jax's mouth fell open. "You want me to work with Ceara?" he gasped. "Uh-ah. You know I'm loyal, yours in life and death and all that, but there are some things that go way beyond my limit."

"What's the matter, bird boy?" Ceara sneered. "Afraid the big, bad Gliss is gonna kick your skinny posterior?"

"Hey, my arse is fine. It's not skinny," Jax protested.

Ceara glanced behind him. "If you say so. I've seen skeletons with finer backsides than you."

Jax glared at Ann. "Why does Ed always get to stay with you?" He crossed his arms. "I'm not useless. I could help during a spell if you needed me to."

"Because I need someone there to anchor me if the spell goes wrong. He's more experienced at doing that than you are."

"She's the only one who can stop him from killing anyone," Ceara added. "That's why it's safer if he stays with her."

"I'm not going to kill anyone." Ed scowled at them. "And I am gaining some control."

Ann took Ed's arm as Ceara and Jax continued to bicker.

"Try not to kill each other," she told them. *Let's go,* she said to Ed.

"While we're on the subject, your arse is..." Jax said.

Ann laughed. "I think deep down they still love each other. They were close when they were younger."

"You sure taking me with you is a good idea?"

"Your beast never threatens me." She slipped her arm through his.

"No, I'm more concerned what I'll do to anyone else it perceives as a threat to you." Ed glanced around, uneasy.

"We'll be fine. I need to work on finding my father's vault and we need to figure out what that thing is that attacked us last night."

They headed away from standing stones and through the forest. Ann raised her hand, forcing the branches aside with her magic. Not many of the druids ever went to the old temple, since the druids themselves didn't worship any gods.

"Are you going to unlock more of my memories?" Ed asked.

"I'll try. You are the only one who recognises that voice." She moved more branches aside, glad when nothing snagged on their clothing.

"I still think it'd be safer if I left," he remarked. "It could have been after me, not you."

"You're not a threat." She breathed in the smell of morning dew and fresh grass. It felt good to be out in nature again. Here, her connection to the earth lines—to Erthea itself—was stronger than in any of the other places she stayed over the past few years.

"Ann, what happens when you're not there to pull me back?" He spun her around to face him. "I don't need innocent blood on my hands."

"You can control this. I know you can." She touched his arm. "That shadow thing is connected to Urien too; I can feel it. Whatever evil they throw at us, we'll face it. Together." She sighed. "I need you with me. I've lost so many people; I can't lose you too." She hugged him.

He'd been her rock all these years. They had a bond that went far deeper than friendship. The three months he'd been held by Orla had been unbearable. She'd find a way to help him and save Xander.

Ed returned her embrace. "I don't want to leave you either, but I'm afraid...of myself." He then pulled back. "Look what I did to Jerome last night. He's lucky he only got a few scratches."

Ann winced. Jerome had barely even looked at her at breakfast earlier. He had avoided her and backed away whenever Ed was near. She felt disappointed. She and Jerome had got close again, but she had more important things to worry about than his feelings being hurt.

"Maybe that's the problem. You're still rejecting your beast side." She pulled away and pushed through the trees.

"Acceptance will be a long time coming," he muttered. "How are you planning on finding the vault?"

"You're not going to like it."

The old temple was a small stone building once used to pay respects to the spirits. Most of the five lands had stopped such worship centuries ago. Trees grew through the empty windows and up through the open rooftop. Vines crept along the barren walls, yet the air still hummed with power.

The earth lines vibrated underneath her feet as she moved though the archway. This place reminded her of the times as children when she and Ed had thought all the buildings left over from ancient times were temples.

Inside, leaves and brambles covered the cracked stone floor. "*Soiléir.*" Ann raised her hand. The leaves and debris were swept away.

At the centre of the room sat a small stone altar. Nothing adorned it now. Three rays of the sun had been carved into it.

"What's the plan then?" Ed asked, leaning back against the altar.

Ann drew a circle on the floor with a piece of chalk. "I'm going to the other side and contacting Xander."

"How does that answer all our questions?" Ed frowned.

"My father always said the other side banished limitations, so over there I should see the door to the vault. Maybe Xander can tell me more about what Urien has planned." She pulled out a vial of black liquid. "I got this from my uncle. It keeps me under, but I need someone to watch over me while I'm gone."

"You still trust me after everything that happened last night?" Ed crossed his arms. "What if Jerome shows up and I attack him again?"

Ann shook her head. "I don't think Jerome will be a problem. Besides, I trust you more than anyone else. You'll be there no matter what. I know that." She laid her cloak out on the floor. "I don't know how long I will be gone." She sat down.

"I'm used to watching you lay dead—it never gets any easier." He stepped into the circle and sat down beside her.

"What are you doing?" Her eyes widened.

"For the sake of keeping my beast happy and in control, I'll stay with you."

She pulled the cork from the vial. "If I don't wake, call Ceara. Gliss are trained to bring the dead back to life."

"You will come back. You always do."

Ann gulped down the poison, feeling its acrid taste in the back of her throat. "Another way to bring me back is to stab me through the heart. It'll force my spirit back into my body once you remove the knife," she said. "Don't do that unless you have to. I'm tired of ruining my clothes, and we can't afford to waste good coin." She felt her heart beat slower and muttered an incantation just before she slumped back into Edward's arms.

Ann reappeared in the gloom of the other side. The blackness seemed thicker every time she came here. This wasn't the final place the dead came to after death. Just a place of transition. She came here every time she almost died—for a while at least, until her body revived itself.

"Xander?" she called. "Xander, are you here?"

No response came.

Okay, I have to make good use of my time here. She moved through the gloom and raised her hand. "Come on, Papa, where did you hide that door?"

Ann saw a flash of the doorway, then it faded. It looked like a simple wooden door surrounded by glowing light. She let it go. She'd come for Xander.

"Whoa, this is odd," Ed remarked as he appeared behind her.

Ann turned and frowned. "What are you doing? You can't be here. You're supposed to be my anchor."

"I didn't do anything. Your spell dragged me." He frowned at the darkness. "Is this where you go every time you die?"

She nodded. "I don't understand how you can be here. The spell is only supposed to work on me." She waved him away. "Go back."

"Does it matter? Maybe I can help while I'm here."

"Ed, I have no idea how the spell could affect you. I can go back thanks to my father's spell, but you—"

"Let's focus on finding Xander. How does he usually appear?" Ed glanced around, looking uneasy.

"I call him, but he doesn't always appear. It's hard because Urien is always repressing him." Ann bit her lip. "I think it's easier when Urien is asleep."

"You, Urien, and Xander are all connected by blood. Focus on that."

She sighed. It wouldn't be that easy. "Urien will still block me."

"You're not calling Urien, you're calling Xander. Try that. Call his spirit." Ed took her hand. "You can do this. Maybe me being here will make you stronger. My beast seems resistant to magic. Damn thing might as well be good for something."

Ann gripped his hand, closed her eyes and muttered words of power to call a spirit. *Spiorad teacht dom.*

Ann knew from experience magic worked differently here—if it worked at all. "I still don't know how you help me focus so well, and yet you can't control your beast." She smiled.

"I'm good at being there for you. Have to be after everything you've been through." He took her hand and his touch tingled. Strange how she could feel it even in spirit form.

"Ann?" Xander appeared in a flash of light. "What are you doing?"

"Xander." She pulled away from Ed and tried to hug her brother, but her arms passed through him. "Xander, you need to tell me what Urien is planning."

"Have you found a way to unbind us?"

Ann shook her head. "No. Tell me how Urien is breaking through the veil. What's he doing?"

"Ann, you need to unbind us. It's the only way to stop him."

"I'm not going to kill you," she snapped.

Xander sighed. "He uses magic—power and spells I've never seen before. He's planned something. A meeting of all the leaders from most of the five lands. It's something big, but he blocks me out to prevent me knowing what. Whatever it is will take place then."

"Think, you must have seen him pierce through the veil. Is he going to kill all the leaders?"

Xander's form flickered.

"No, you can't go." Ann's hand flared with power as she tried to grab hold of his spirit.

"Unbind us. It's the only way."

Her eyes narrowed. "Urien."

He laughed. "Didn't think I'd let our traitorous little brother help you so easily, did you, sister? I'll never give up Xander's body." He glared at Edward. "Not unless you give me my own body back." He vanished in a flash of light.

CHAPTER 16

Ed opened his eyes and found himself back in the temple. His head throbbed, no doubt from being dragged to the other side along with Ann. He looked down to see Ann's head still resting on his lap. Her eyes were still closed, and he couldn't hear her heartbeat. "Ann? Ann, wake up."

She didn't respond.

"Ann." Ed shook her harder this time. "Wake up."

Damn it, had Urien done something to her? His heart pounded in his ears. He had always feared one day she wouldn't wake up, and the spell meant to protect her from death would no longer work.

She'd told him to call Ceara if she didn't wake up, but that would take too long. Checking her neck, he felt no sign of a pulse, nor could he hear her heartbeat.

Ed opened her mouth and breathed air into her, pressing on her chest to try and get her heart to start working again. "Come on, breathe. I'm not losing you to him."

After a few moments, Ann coughed and opened her eyes.

"Let's not cross over again any time soon." Ed slumped back against the wall.

Ann clutched her head. "Urien used magic to try and trap me there." She glanced around. "How did you know how to revive me?"

"I've learnt a few things from the Gliss." He didn't elaborate on that. All past experiences with the Gliss were best forgotten.

She sighed as she sat up. "I'm still no closer to finding that vault." She pushed her hair off her face. "Damn, for a moment I thought I'd glimpsed it earlier."

"I don't think you should contact Xander again. We have no way of knowing if it's him or Urien."

"But Xander is still alive. He's trapped in there." She picked up her cloak and wrapped it around herself. "So much for getting answers."

"Who says we can't get more answers? Cast the spell again. If I can find out what that thing was, maybe we can figure out what Urien's next move is."

Ann hesitated. "You've just passed over, a spell—"

"I'll be fine. The beast makes me stronger." He lay down, struggling to get into a comfortable position as the cold floor seeped into his back.

"You are too stubborn for your own good, you big lug." She smiled down at him, placing her hands on the side of his head.

Ann said the familiar words of the incantation.

Let me go deeper, he thought. *Come on, beast, you can help me remember.*

The magic dragged him under, and he found himself back surrounded by the blue trees. The air smelled crisp and fresh, the scents of grass and flowers filling his lungs.

This again.

Ann appeared beside him. "I've never seen trees like these before," she said. "We must be somewhere in Asral, or maybe Lulrien."

Parts of those lands had been cut off for centuries. Years of war had destroyed parts of the continent of Almara and left them cut off. Legend stated those lands had been left uninhabitable, much like the wasteland between Asral and Vala.

Yet here they appeared in his memory. *Why do I keep coming back here? Why is this place so important?*

"This place must be important," Ann mused. "Perhaps you used to live near here, or it was somewhere you came to regularly."

"I'm not going to even ask how you heard that," he said.

"We're connected by the spell, silly." She gave him a nudge.

"Right, then how did I end up being dragged over to the other side with you?" Ed raised a brow.

She shrugged. "You and I have a bond after everything we've been through. I'm the one who found you when you washed up on Trin."

Yes, they did have a bond that went much deeper than mere friendship. He knew her better than he knew himself at times.

"Nothing is happening," he observed.

"You're still trying too hard." She smirked.

Ed rolled his eyes. "Why did I forget all this? It makes no sense. I was old enough to have memories when I landed on Trin."

"Could be trauma from almost drowning, or maybe something bad happened to you," Ann said. "It's hard for the mind to keep reliving bad things. Believe me, I know."

"Yeah, but you dealt with it." He squeezed her hand.

The trees blurred as he moved through the woods. The image of them became less focused, and he could no longer smell the scents he had before.

What was that thing that chased me? Come on, I need to remember.

"Relax," Ann said. "Close your eyes."

"We're inside my mind. What good will that do here?"

"Just do it, you big lug."

He did so. Images flashed in front of him. People and faces that felt familiar, yet he had no recollection of who they were, or how they were related to him. Who were they? His brow creased in concentration. The harder he tried to focus on the faces, the dimmer the images became. "I used to play here and climbed trees. The beast…" Ed frowned. "It was part of me. It doesn't feel like a separate entity."

"Did you have any family?"

Ed shook his head. "I don't think so." Every time he thought of family, images of Flo, Ann, Jax, and the rest of the Black came to mind.

"Okay, maybe you're focusing on too many things at once. Just focus on the events before you jumped into the sea," she suggested. "What were you running from?"

Ed found himself back running through the forest. Branches caught at his shirt and trousers.

Light blurred behind, he could almost make out the silhouette of a person but couldn't make out if they were male or female.

"Why are they chasing you?"

Ed's brow creased in confusion.

Ann? Ed? Jax's voice echoed around them. *Ann, we need you.*

Ed opened his eyes and pulled himself away from the memory. *What's wrong, Jax?*

There are Gliss on their way to the village. Did you find what you were looking for?

Not exactly, he replied.

We're on our way, Ann said, scrambling up and grabbing her cloak. She yanked it back on.

"I can get us back there faster if I carry you," Ed suggested.

"Alright." She wrapped her arms around his neck as he picked her up.

They reappeared back at the village a few moments later. "Whoa, I think I preferred that more when I had a concussion." Ann swayed a little as he set her down on her feet. "I don't see Urien or Xander here."

"Since when does he ever fight his own battles?" Ed spotted a Gliss coming toward them. He pulled Ann out of the way as a throwing knife came at them.

Ann drew her own knives. *And so the fun begins.*

Ed felt his beast at the edge of his mind, clawing to get out and take control.

Ed snarled as a Gliss lunged at him. *When will they ever learn?* He blocked the Gliss's blow and sent her flying as the beast took over. All at once, the world around him changed. Everything seemed to become brighter, louder, more vivid than before.

Another Gliss threw a knife. It hissed through the air. Ed dodged it before it had a chance to come near him.

The other druid warriors all stood trying to fight off more Gliss as they came swarming through.

Jax appeared, swinging his staff and slicing into two Gliss as they came at him.

Ed growled as a Gliss jumped him from behind, prodding a metal rod into his neck. Static jolted through him, the pain barely registered. He spun around, grabbed the weapon, and crushed it as his fingers curled around it.

Ed, keep one of them alive for me, Ann called.

He turned to stare at her in disbelief. The Gliss took the advantage of the distraction and jabbed the rod against the side of his head.

Ed fell to his knees as pain tore through his skull. It made his head feel like it would explode.

Ann ran over, spun and kicked the Gliss, sending the other woman stumbling.

Ignoring the agony, Ed leapt up, grabbed the Gliss by the throat and snapped her neck.

"Thanks," he muttered. *But why would you want to keep a Gliss alive? Isn't having one Gliss supposedly on our side enough?*

Because— Ann got cut off as two Gliss lunged at them.

Ed blocked the next blow and proceeded to kill the next Gliss who tried to put him down.

The four of them fought together, taking each Gliss down one by one.

Ed watched Ann knock down the last Gliss. "Keep this one alive," she told them.

The Gliss shot up, coming at Ann with a knife.

Ceara threw her own knife, hitting the other Gliss in the throat.

"I told you to keep her alive," Ann snapped.

"The only good Gliss is a dead one," Ceara replied. "Why would you want one anyway?"

"For information. We still don't know where Urien's meeting will be held." Ann sighed and pushed her long hair off her face.

"You'll never be able to break a Gliss," Ed pointed out.

"I could," Ceara retorted. "But it would take time. If you really want to get to Urien, there is another way of doing it."

CHAPTER 17

Ann stood at the centre of the standing stones. Their power vibrated unharmed against her skin. Their energy still felt strong, but not strong as it could be. Every few decades, the archdruid had to reset their power. Darius had shown her how to do it, but she'd never attempted the spell before now. She'd never needed to.

Strange. Back then, Ann had thought Darius would be around forever. She thought it would be years before she'd have to do this. But now Ann would have to reinforce the magic. It'd be the only way to ensure the druids' survival.

Ann took a deep breath then sensed someone coming toward her. Jerome.

She turned around as he came over.

"It's good being back here, isn't it?" he asked. "We've been so long without the power of the archdruid."

She flinched at that. "You know I won't stay here forever. I never stay in one place too long. It's safer that way."

"But you could be safe here. This is where you belong, Rhiannon."

Ann shook her head. "A lot has changed over the past few years," she pointed out. "Rhiannon died that night, too."

"But why can't you stay? You'd be safe here. With the stones and strength of our people…it would be enough to keep you and everyone here safe." Jerome took her hand.

It felt strange to hold hands with anyone except for Edward. She and Ed had been holding hands since they were children, so it felt natural with him.

"Because I'm still accused of murdering my parents. I am a so-called traitor and wanted fugitive throughout the five lands. If I stay, people would only keep trying to come for me." She pulled her hand away. "I'm sorry. Believe me, I wish things could be different."

"We could help keep you safe like your guards do. And like that Gliss."

She laughed. "Ed and Jax haven't been my guards for a long time. They're my friends."

"Edward is just a friend?"

Ann frowned. "Why do you keep asking me that? I never understood why you never liked Ed. He's a good man."

"He was with you almost all the time when we were a couple."

"That was his job as one of the Black." She tapped her foot, impatient to get this conversation over with.

"I guess I wanted you all to myself. I loved you very much. Those feelings have never gone away."

"Ed is my best friend, my partner. More than that. I doubt I would have got through the past few years without him," Ann admitted. "There's nothing romantic between us. Nor can I promise you a real relationship. My life is too complicated for that."

"Then I guess we'd better enjoy whatever time we have left together."

"While you're here, maybe you can help me reinforce the power of the stones." She held out her hand for him and he took it. Having the power of another druid with her would help.

Energy sizzled between them as the power of his own earth affinity combined with her firepower.

Ann chanted words of power, the spell that would restore the stones and replenish their strength. *"Na clocha a athbhunú agus a neartú."*

Light flared around the circle for a moment then vanished.

Her frown deepened. "That's not supposed to happen."

Why hadn't it worked? Darius had made sure she learned the important spells by heart. She'd practiced them for days at a time.

Darius had made this spell look easy. The last time he'd reinforced the stones' power she'd been around him. It had been fifteen years since then, and their energy had remained strong.

"I don't understand why it wouldn't work," she said, more to herself than Jerome.

Jerome wrapped an arm around her. "Maybe you need all of us. You should perform a circle tonight and you can reinforce the circle and your bond with our people."

"A circle?" Her eyes widened.

Her father rarely performed circles with the other druids. He said he'd never seen the need. But then Darius had been different from other archdruids of the past. Far removed from the druid people.

Ann had never performed a joint circle with other druids. Only ever with her father or close family members.

Most druids preferred to cast their own circles alone.

"Yes, it's a perfect opportunity to do it. Tonight is the full moon, after all." Jerome smiled. "Perhaps afterwards we can spend time together tonight."

"Maybe," she agreed.

"I think a circle is the perfect idea," Sage remarked as Ann sat in Sage's new house. It hadn't taken Sage long to get her own lodging and make it home; they had only been in Trewa for a couple of weeks.

"But I've never led a circle, and I'm not their—I'm not the archdruid they want me to be." She sighed and sipped her tea. "Blaise has been their leader for years. I feel like an outsider."

"It's going to take more than a few days to adjust to life here." Sage patted her hand.

"Jerome thinks I should stay here."

"Do you want to?" Sage poured herself some tea and sipped it.

"I don't know. I've moved around so much since my parents died." She shook her head. "I guess I've grown used to it. Besides, how is staying a possibility? Nothing's changed. I'm still a rogue—a fugitive. As are the others. I don't want to put innocent lives at risk."

"If you restore the stones to their full strength, I don't see why you couldn't stay," Sage replied. "I'd be glad to have you, as would Blaise."

"I doubt that. He's made his feelings clear."

"Give Blaise some time. He and Darius had a difficult relationship."

Ann sipped her tea, wishing for something stronger. The idea of settling and having a real home again still seemed impossible.

"You should be careful with Jerome too," Sage added.

"Why? He hasn't done anything to make me not trust him." The thought of them spending the night together still made her stomach flutter.

"I meant with his feelings. That man loved you."

Ann waved a hand. "We were only together a few weeks. Besides, I don't believe in romance. How can you vow to love someone for the rest of your life?" She scoffed. "Nothing lasts forever. Certainly not romantic love."

"Flora and I were together for thirty years. I fell in love with her the moment I saw her." Sage smiled, eyes glistening. "Sometimes things will be hard, and you have to fight for it. But love can and does last." Sage brushed away a tear. "I meant you should be careful with Jerome because of Edward."

Ann rolled her eyes. "Why does everyone think we're a couple? We're not. He's my partner, my person. Now *that's* a love that will last forever. It has nothing to do with romance." She gulped down the rest of her tea.

"I know your father wasn't faithful to anyone. You shouldn't let that stop you from finding happiness."

"Sage, I don't have time for romance. I have to save my brother and the five lands." She stood up. "See you at the circle. I still don't understand why the spell didn't work."

"There can be many reasons why a spell doesn't work. Usually it has to do with the one casting it."

"I accept my role as archdruid, even if I don't like it. There's no reason why it shouldn't work." She moved around the table and touched Sage's shoulder. "See you later. No doubt you'll be there to make sure I don't screw up tonight."

Ann fumbled with her long white robe. Sage had somehow found one for her and insisted she wear it that night. The robe proved to be more of a dress, it had a long neckline and a black underskirt with slits that ran up to her thighs. It even had a hood—which was good, since she missed her cloak. She felt naked and exposed in this outfit. Nothing like herself. The straps of her leather corset showed, so she pulled the dress up to cover them.

Ann hadn't worn a dress in five years. She'd been forced to wear heavy cumbersome gowns during her father's rule.

Ceara came in. "Wow, you look like the archdruid now."

"I feel naked. Why can't I just wear my usual clothes?" She rubbed her bare arms and glanced down at her cloak.

"At least they're not making you go sky clad. You'd be naked then." Ceara laughed.

"Shouldn't you be resting?" It'd only been a few days since Ann had managed to stop Urien's spell from killing Ceara. She had more colour in her cheeks now, but still needed some recovery time.

Ceara scowled. "No, Jax and I are on wolf watch tonight."

"Wolf watch?" Ann frowned, having no idea what she meant.

"Hello, full moon. Ed gets edgy from what Jax told me, and you won't be there to calm him."

"I can't be with Ed all the time. But I'm sure he'll be fine."

"Aren't you and Jerome supposed to be spending the night together?" Ceara waggled her eyebrows.

"No, we're going for a walk after the circle. Maybe having a drink together." She didn't feel like talking about her arrangement with Jerome later. In truth, she had no idea what would happen yet.

"If that's not an invitation for sex, then I don't know what is." Ceara's grin faded. "How can you even consider it?"

"It's been awhile since I had any. Jerome is—"

"He isn't Ed. Have you thought for one moment how he'll feel watching you go off somewhere?" The Gliss crossed her arms.

Ann rolled her eyes. "Why does everyone keep suggesting we're a couple?"

"Because you are, even if you don't have sex. You're more than friends."

"Yes, but we're not lovers. We never will be. He's my—well, he's not that." She grew weary of keep having to explain her relationship with Edward to everyone.

"Yes, but his beast says you're his. Doesn't that mean something to you?"

"Should it?" She ran a brush through her long hair.

Ceara heaved a sigh. "You're never going admit how you feel about him, are you?"

"I already know how I feel about Ed. I trust him more than anyone."

"Why can't you—?"

"I'll see you in the morning." Ann stalked out of the room, heart pounding more than ever.

She felt nervous enough about the circle. Now Ceara made her feel anxious about the possibility of spending the night with Jerome. And for what?

She and Ed had never been anything more than friends.

Ann headed straight to Ed's cabin and found him pacing up and down. The room looked similar to her own, with little more than a table, two chairs and two makeshift beds.

His eyes widened as she walked in. "You look—"

"Ridiculous, I know." She let go of the hem of her skirt.

"I was going to say beautiful."

She smiled. "Are you sure you'll be alright?" Every full moon, his beast side grew more restless than usual. It demanded control, and so far they hadn't been able to keep it under control during this time of the month. Full moons were the worst time for him.

"I'll be fine. Don't worry about me." He waved a hand in dismissal. "Go, enjoy the circle."

Ann bit her lip. "I'm worried it won't work. I still don't feel connected to these people like I thought I would." She wrapped her arms around herself. "I'm an outsider." She paused, biting her lip harder. "Jerome asked me to stay. He thinks we could stay here and be safe."

Ed stopped pacing. "I don't think that's a good idea. We're still rogues, and we have large prices on our heads."

She nodded. "I know. If I can reinforce the stones, maybe we could stay."

"If that's what you want, then do it."

"Will you stay?" She reached out and touched his shoulder. After five years on the run together, she couldn't imagine being apart from him again.

Ed shrugged. "Maybe. I need to find out where I came from, though. If there are other lykaes out there, then I may leave at some point."

"I should go. It's getting dark and the moon will be up soon." She turned to leave. "Ed, does seeing me with Jerome bother you?" She felt surprised to hear the words coming out of her mouth.

Ed flinched. "Why…why would it? We're not a couple. And you deserve to be happy."

Ann breathed a sigh of relief. "Right. I don't know what I—I should go." She wrapped her arms around him in an attempt to ease the awkwardness. "You know where I am if you need me tonight."

Ed pulled her close, and the warmth of his body enveloped her. His embrace felt welcoming, safe. As if she could happily stay there forever.

She pulled away, reminding herself it would be Jerome she'd be spending the night with. "I'll see you later," she added.

"Don't be nervous. You can do the spell."

She smiled. "Who says I'm nervous?"

"I feel it—and your heart is racing."

"Well, wish me luck."

"Good luck with the circle…and Jerome."

Ann's nerves grew as she headed toward the standing stones. She didn't want to think about what might happen if the spell didn't work.

What if I remembered the spell wrong? Maybe that's why it didn't work. Her hands clenched. *Get a grip,* she told herself. *An archdruid doesn't panic or run away.*

Ann had been trained to be the archdruid since early childhood. She'd been born for this, or else she wouldn't have been given the power. Even Darius hadn't chosen her to be his heir. Either you got the power, or you didn't.

I can do this. Ann glanced back. She wished Ed could be there. Then she'd have his strength to support her. She'd be able to make sure he stayed in control.

Argh, Ed and I can't be together all the time. It's not natural. Just stay calm. Remember you can do this. Ann forced her face to remain impassive as she approached the stones. To her surprise, more druids than she'd seen living in the village had gathered within the circle.

No doubt Sage had called them.

Oh blessed spirits, I'll have more people to—

Blaise appeared at her side, cutting off her panic.

She raised a brow. "I didn't expect to see you here."

"I'm a druid. If you need me to help reinforce the power of the stones, I'll be there," Blaise said. "I hope your lykae is under control tonight."

"He's not my—why do you say that?" Her eyes narrowed. She'd been wondering whether Blaise knew more about lykaes than he let on, but trying to pry information out of her uncle had proved futile.

He and Darius were more alike than Blaise thought.

"The full moon can affect lykaes. With all these people gathered—"

"He won't hurt anyone," she insisted.

"He already injured Jerome," Blaise pointed out.

"He didn't...he is learning to control it."

Ed had been managing to control the beast better since he started training. Like with her magic, control would come with time.

Ann moved to the centre of the crowd, pulling her hood up as she went. Her heart thudded against her ribs. No doubt Ed would be able to hear it from wherever he was.

"Thank you all for coming tonight," her voice came out stronger than expected. "We're gathered here to—"

"Why should we trust you?" A dark-haired man spoke up and glared at her. "Some here believe you killed your father for his power."

Her heart sank as she gritted her teeth. This she hadn't expected.

Ann had grown used to the rumours and accusations over the years. But she'd thought her father's people would at least believe her innocence.

"I never killed my parents. I tried to save my father that night." She forced her voice to stay calm.

"You've been running ever since that night," a woman spoke up. "If you are innocent, why run?"

Another woman spoke up: "A true archdruid would have come to be with her people. You treat us with contempt and abandoned us just like your father did."

Ann's heart twisted. Power bubbled up from deep inside her as it often did when she felt strong emotion. Her eyes flashed with golden light.

"I never killed my parents—my brother did. This is my truth. I swear this by blood vow." One of her knives appeared in her hand and she pricked her finger with it. She let drops of blood drip onto the ground. A blood vow was binding. If she lied, the magic would rebound and possibly kill her.

"It was my brother Urien and his mother Orla who killed my parents." Ann kept her voice even. "I never came here because I thought I'd be putting your lives at risk. I ran because I had to." She pushed her hair back. "There's a greater power that helped Urien and Orla take control of Caselhelm. I haven't been able to identify it yet. I spent the past five years helping those hunted by Orla. I work with the resistance now and help other rogues like me who don't have a place within the five lands." She paused. "My brother is back, and Orla has been hunting our people to extinction, but I'm here now, and I will reinforce the power of the stones."

The crowd fell silent.

"Unless anyone else has any objections, let's begin," Ann added. The cut on her finger faded.

Everyone moved, joining hands as they formed a circle within the ring of stones.

Sage moved to Ann's side and flashed her a grin. "Told you that you had it in you," she whispered. Sage's gnarled fingers closed around hers.

Ann took a deep breath and began to recite words of power. "*Cad a briseadh agus a cuireadh ar ais, lig an t-iomlán arís,*" she recited.

Energy rose within the circle, starting within the druids themselves. Every man and woman took on different coloured energy as their powers flared to life.

A cool breeze whipped around the stones as energy began to build.

Ann recited the words again, feeling her own power rise in unison with theirs.

The stones themselves hummed, vibrating with their ethereal blue glow. Sound rang out as the power within the circle of druids bounced against each stone. The light hovered there a moment before it faded away.

Her stomach dropped. It hadn't worked. She could feel it in the vibration of the stones. Their energy had been made stronger, but not as strong as it should have been.

Someone clapped, and people began to congratulate her and thank her for her help.

Ann drew away. She didn't want praise. She'd failed to restore both the stones and as the archdruid.

CHAPTER 18

Urien paced up and down the length of his study. He'd instructed his mother to gather together the leaders from around Almara. He would make a stand, to convince them he, not Ann, was the true archdruid. But most hadn't responded yet.

Why would anyone want you? You're nothing. Just a parasite inside someone else's body, Xander said.

Urien grabbed a jug of ale and chugged it down. It tasted sharp, but he needed it. *Gods, I've got to find a way to block him out. Or better yet, get rid of him once and for all.*

He had to find a way to draw Ann out into the open. Even he wasn't strong enough to break through the power of the stones at

Trewa. He could send Gliss, banelings, and other creatures, but they would only do so much good. He needed a way to truly force her out.

Summoning the leaders would do just that but it would have to seem like a true threat.

"I need power," he muttered. "I need allies if I'm gonna get what I want."

The door opened.

Urien spun around and growled, "I said I wasn't to be disturbed."

The Ursaie woman looked up, startled. "Your mother told me to bring your potion."

Another slave came in carrying a tray of food.

Urien muttered a curse and grabbed the second slave by the arm. He remembered what the shadow creature had said: "Blood is power."

He sliced his dagger across her throat and muttered words of power. *"Nochtann bóthair i bhfolach."* Power pulsed from her body.

The other Ursaie screamed and dropped the potion. It clattered to the floor and sloshed its contents everywhere.

"Stay," Urien commanded. His vision blurred and his head spun. Dizziness rolled over him like a ship rocking back and forth.

Light flashed in front of his eyes as a door appeared. Old, wooden, illuminated by green light.

He reached out to touch it. Heat flared against his skin. The runes flashed with power, repelling him. A blast of energy sent him stumbling backward. *No, mine!* Urien shot forward, grabbing for the door a second time. Buzzing roared through his ears and heat seared against his flesh.

"Let me pass," he muttered. *I'm in Xander's body. Let me through.*

Why wouldn't it let him through? He had Xander's body. The magic shouldn't resist him. Heat seared his fingers as he touched the door. Even Xander cried out in pain.

Let go! Xander shouted. *You can't go through.*

I will get through, Urien muttered more words of power.

A burst of energy sent him hurtling across the room. The door vanished and the power from the Ursaie's body faded.

Urien slumped to the floor, resting his head against the wall. His chest rose and fell with rasping breaths. Welts covered his skin from where he had touched the door. *Why didn't it work? Why didn't your worthless body work?*

Xander remained silent. Strange, Urien had been so desperate to silence him, but now he would have welcomed a response.

A whimpering sound caught his attention. The other slave cowered in the corner. She trembled as his spell held her in place.

Power hummed from deep inside her. More untapped power.

"Come…here," Urien ordered.

Her body shook harder as she rose and walked over. "Please don't—"

Urien shot up, slicing the blade across her throat. Normally he enjoyed people's pleas for help, but not this time. Her body went limp in his arms. Power rolled out of her as her life faded away.

Urien chanted more words of power, letting her magic flow through Xander's body. Warmth washed over him.

"Seanóirí, mé ag ceiliúradh ort."

No wonder the Ursaie were condemned. Their power felt incredible.

Magic vibrated through the air as he recited the words again.

Work, please work. Urien waited, unsure if anyone would answer his call.

"Come on, answer me," he muttered. "I need your help."

Both slaves lay on the floor, discarded. Blood gathered on the hardwood, mixing with the contents of the splattered potion.

Orbs of light flashed as a dark-haired man with electric blue eyes materialised. He wore a long grey tunic, and grey trousers. His brilliant blue eyes narrowed as he sneered, "Who are you to summon me?"

"I'm—"

"I know who you are. You're the bastard of that demon witch Orla."

"You're Arwan, an elder, aren't you?" Urien said. Gods, it had worked. He almost wanted to jump for joy.

"I am, but I don't know why you would dare summon me," Arwan snapped. "Your mother already failed to keep her promise to us five years ago. We are not interested in—"

"Wait." Urien held up his hand to silence him. "I am here to make a new offer."

Arwan laughed. "What could you possibly offer me, boy? You are nothing."

"I am the rightful archdruid." Urien cast his arms. "It's my birthright. I am Darius' first-born child."

"That power is not ours to give. Your sister is the archdruid. She is bound by us."

"Know that if you help me defeat her, I'll take her power from her. I'll be like the archdruids of old," Urien said. "I'll answer to the elders. Be your faithful servant."

Arwan snorted. "Your sister is more powerful than you. Why would we want you?"

Urien's jaw clenched as he fought to control his anger. He couldn't afford to lose his temper around this man. "Ann would never answer to the elders. Our father turned her against you long before I killed him," he said. "Oh, she knows the elders exist, but she's a rogue, just like Darius. You can't hope to sway her to your side." He felt Xander's presence returning. Damn, the blood magic had been strong enough to mute him. Why couldn't it have lasted longer?

He couldn't show any signs of weakness, or it would ruin any chance of an alliance, and any hope he had of getting what he truly wanted.

"And what good could you do?" Arwan demanded. "Your sister is an enemy, yes, but we wouldn't say no to having her power on our side."

"Help me and I'll take her power and her life," Urien promised. "I know how much the elders need an archdruid working with them rather than against them." He paused. "I'll arrange a meeting demanding every leader in the five lands come here. Even those who live beyond the mists."

"And?" Arwan raised an eyebrow.

"I'll do it under the guise of being the archdruid. Think, it's the perfect opportunity to bring your enemies together—those who don't answer to the elders."

"What makes you think we need your help? We are gods, after all. We can kill whomever we choose."

"What do you want, then?" Urien demanded. He was running out of ideas. If the deaths of a dozen people wouldn't help, nor the promise of a new archdruid, what would?

Arwan paced, wrinkling his nose at the sight of the dead slaves. "It's true, things would be easier if we had an archdruid. Thanks to your sister, the resistance is proving to be a nuisance. But you could gain favour again if you did something for us."

Urien bit back a smile, barely able to contain his excitement. "Name it." Whatever they wanted, he would do it. Orla had failed in her chance of gaining true favour from the elders. He wouldn't make the same mistake.

"If you could trap your sister and hand her over to us, we'd make you the next archdruid, as you desire."

No, Xander cried. *You can't do that. You have no idea what they'll do to her.*

"Consider it done. I'll find a way to do just that." This time, he let the grin spread across his face and his eyes lit up with excitement.

"You'd better. Don't waste our time again." Arwan vanished in a swirl of light.

Urien stepped over the bodies and hurried into the secret chamber. He moved through the living space and opened another door into a smaller room. Darius had used this space to practice his private magic in.

Urien rummaged through the different artefacts. It had to be here somewhere. He'd seen Darius use the device before, a large crystal orb that allowed him to contact all the different leaders of the five lands. Urien didn't know why he hadn't thought of it earlier. With one call, he could arrange the meeting and demand every leader come to the palace. Some of them might refuse, but Urien had seen Darius telling Ann about the device. It held magic that would compel the recipient to answer the call.

Everything in this room had been left as it was when Darius died. Urien had no idea how his father had managed to find anything; the entire place seemed like organised chaos rather than neat and orderly.

He moved stacks of parchment and opened different boxes as he went. Darius had several orbs, but not the one he'd seen Darius and Ann using before.

Where is it?

Where is what? Xander asked. *What are you looking for?*

Do shut up, Urien snapped. *Now I know blood magic can silence you, I'll start killing more slaves if you don't be quiet.*

No, don't do that! He sensed Xander's panic and bit back a smile. Good, perhaps he finally had a way of keeping his brother in line now.

Urien shoved aside several books, knocking them to the floor. Dust rose like mist as they hit the ground. He coughed, covered his nose, then his eyes widened. Sitting there on a large pedestal was a dark black orb. Next to it lay another stone. It glittered like a large diamond etched with ancient signals. *No, it can't be.* Surely Darius wouldn't have been foolish enough to leave such a valuable weapon lying around? But then maybe he hadn't had time to hide everything away.

He grabbed it, feeling power crackle against his fingers. *This is it. This is an elder device. We don't have things like it here on Erthea.* He picked up the stone with his other hand. Finally, he would have true power. No more wasting time trying to recruit people. He'd have an army of his own.

Urien placed the orb on the table. How had Darius activated it? With a spell?

No, blood. Blood magic would make it work. Blood magic had proved stronger than anything so far. Drawing his blade, he pricked his finger and watched Xander's blood drip onto the orb. The orb flared with power, humming with energy.

"I, the archdruid Urien Valeran, demand all leaders within the five lands come to the palace at Larenth." He smirked as his blood sizzled against the orb. The orb pulsed with white light. He knew one way or another the magic would have its desired effect.

Urien clutched the stone. Now it was time to recruit an army even more valuable than anything Caselhelm had to offer. More slaves to do his bidding. Only these ones wouldn't have a choice. With this stone, they would have no choice but to obey him. For the first time in centuries, the wyvern race would be under his control again.

CHAPTER 19

Ed paced the length his cabin until the walls felt like they were closing in on him. Jax and Ceara sat around the table. Their stares and silent scrutiny only set him more on edge.

"I'm going for a walk," Ed told them. "I can't stay here any longer."

"You can't. If you go out, you might attack someone." Ceara rested her boots on the table and chugged back some ale.

"I won't. I just—I need to be outside."

"You could find a nice woman to hook up with," Ceara suggested.

"I doubt that's a good idea." Jax glowered at her. "He might attack someone if he loses control."

"Why? Ann is getting busy tonight. Maybe we should follow her example, and all have some fun."

"Well done for reminding him," Jax hissed under his breath.

Ed resumed pacing. The beast growled, clawing at the cage of his mind.

He didn't want to think about Ann with Jerome.

"Spirits, why did I give her my blessing?" he muttered. "She asked me if I was okay with her and Jerome."

"You've only got yourself to blame for that one, wolfy." Ceara chugged more beer.

"Sister dearest, do you have a compassionate bone in your body?" Jax nudged her. "We're supposed to support Ed, not make him feel worse."

"Here's an idea: why don't you tell Ann how you feel? Then she wouldn't go for Jerome." Ceara set her tankard down. "And I was supportive. I told Ann she should admit how she feels about you. But as per usual, neither of you will admit the truth."

"I can't tell her." Ed sighed. "I tried earlier, and I can't be with her or anyone. I can barely control myself."

"But you love her, right?" Jax prompted.

"I—" he hissed out a breath. "I'm going for a run." Ed blurred out the door before either of them could say another word.

Running and being outside seemed to help a little during the full moon.

He couldn't always be with Ann to keep the beast calm. Sooner or later, he knew he'd have to leave. The thought of leaving her and the others made his stomach twist.

Ed stopped and inhaled, taking in all the scents around him. The sweet scent—like honey—of magic filled the air.

Ann would be doing her circle. Soon the power of the stones would be restored. He had no doubt she could do it. Not because she was the archdruid, but because she was the strongest person he knew. After that, she'd be off with Jerome. The thought sickened him.

Rage heated his blood once more. His fangs came out, along with his claws, as the moon's power beat down on him. He stared up at the glowing white orb. Its strength forced the change. Something he'd been fighting all night.

Spirits, he hoped he could keep the beast under control.

He pushed all thought of Ann and Jerome out of his mind. Instead, Ed ran, blurring away from the village. Trees rushed by, dark and foreboding as he moved. The movement seemed to appease the beast. He inhaled again; hunting prey would help, too.

Ed heard the scurrying of forest creatures as he listened. Rabbits, birds, rodents. All of them scurried by.

Ed, where are you? Jax called. *Now isn't the time to go running off.*

He's probably gone off to slaughter Jerome, Ceara remarked.

Don't put ideas in his head.

Ed growled at the mention of Jerome. Even if he did want to slaughter him, he wouldn't do it. He'd never killed in cold blood before. That would only hurt Ann. He could never do that.

The sound of flapping wings caught his attention as the trees overhead bent under the force of a gale.

His eyes stung as dust and dirt whipped around him. *What's that?* Ed had never seen anything that big before. *That's no bird.* No Magickind could have wings like that.

Ed blurred, following the shadow. If whatever it was wanted to harm the druids, it'd be in for a shock.

The beast perked up. Finally, it had something challenging to hunt.

Trees rushed past. He kept to the shadows as he went, careful not to spook whatever creature it was. Ed growled as more dust stung his eyes. *Quiet,* he told the beast. *Do you want it to hear us?*

The wind picked up as the looming shadow flew fast overhead. Damn, if that shadow was the thing that attacked Ann before, he'd bloody well make it suffer.

Ed moved faster, keeping pace with it. As he entered a clearing, the shape became clearer. An enormous beast with a wide wingspan of at least twenty feet loomed overhead. Its eyes glimmered like fire.

What is that? Ed wondered. Excitement flooded through him— although it was hard to tell if it came from him or the beast.

Ed blurred as the creature swooped down and landed in front of him. It roared.

That's a wyvern. He remembered Flora telling him stories about them when he was a boy. They were supposed to be a myth.

Ed snarled, bearing his own fangs. His beast didn't want to run— even if he did.

216

The wyvern shook its head and let out a mournful cry. A metal collar surrounded its neck. It glowed with runes.

Ed hesitated as the creature continued to stare at him. Why didn't his own beast want to attack? This thing was meant to be prey, yet his beast felt calm, sad even. The emotion formed in his chest.

The beast could feel sad? Or could he somehow sense the wyvern's emotions?

The wyvern let out another cry. Its serpentine head craned toward him. Its golden eyes glistened—with tears.

Tears? Why would it cry? This beast was stronger than any Magickind he'd seen before.

"What's wrong?" Ed's voice came out low and guttural. "Why are you crying? Don't you want to kill me?" He took a deep breath, but his own beast refused to retreat.

The wyvern let out another low wail.

Ed doubled over, clutching his head as pain exploded inside his skull. Deep mournful wailing rang through his ears.

"Argh, spirits, stop," Ed cried. All at once the sound faded.

The wyvern stood there, unmoving, staring. "What do you want?" Ed asked. "Are you trying to communicate with me?"

Slowly, the wyvern nodded. Its neck craned as it reached for him.

Ed reached out, feeling the rough scales along its head. *Why aren't you attacking?* he said to his own beast. *What does it mean?*

"Are you a prisoner?" Ed asked, touching the collar. Its runes flared to life, humming with power. "Is that why you're here? Do you need help?"

The wyvern snorted out a breath. Ed had no idea if that meant yes or no.

"It'd be easier if you could talk," he remarked. "Maybe you're just find trying to find some peace tonight, too, huh? Does the moon hold sway over you, too?"

The wyvern's head snapped back, and it screamed. The runes on its collar flashed.

Ed backed away. "If you're here to hurt the druids, I will stop you," he hissed, fangs bared.

The wyvern took to the air, its massive wings flapping as it flew off into the distance. Ed watched it. The creature headed in the opposite direction, away from Trewa.

What had it wanted? Why even come here?

Ann. Spirits, what if Urien had sent it?

How could I be so careless? Ed blurred back; his thoughts focused solely on Ann. He stopped when he spotted her walking away from the village. Jerome trailed after her.

"Rhiannon, what's wrong?" Jerome asked. "The circle went just as planned. We should—"

"Please just leave me alone," she said, covering her face with her hands. "I'm sorry, I can't stay with you tonight."

"Why not? Ann, please—"

Light sparkled around her as she transported herself away.

Heat flared through his blood again.

Not again. The rage had returned. *Not now!* Why did this keep happening? Was it the moon, or something else?

The need to hunt and kill threatened to overwhelm him.

Strange, the beast had been calm when he'd been with the wyvern. Had a potential threat to Ann caused it?

Jerome turned as if sensing Ed's presence.

Ed gritted his teeth, his fangs digging in. *No*, he thought. *I'm not hunting druids. I need to find Ann.* He didn't have to search; he could feel her close by in the grove. Ed blurred, reappearing in front of her.

"Ed, what are you doing?" She wiped a stray tear off her cheek. "I thought you were—"

Pain wrenched inside his chest—her pain. He winced and the beast retreated. Ed doubled over, breathing hard.

"Ed? I thought you locked yourself up tonight?" Ann moved closer.

"I did but it drove me mad, so I came out for a run," he explained. "I saw a wyvern."

Ann's mouth fell open. "What? That's not possible."

"Well, I saw it."

"Did it attack you?" She touched his shoulder and looked him over for injuries.

"No, I think it tried to talk to me. I don't know if it's a threat." He shook his head. "I came to check on you—in case it came back."

"Why would a wyvern come here?"

Ed shrugged. "No idea. How did the circle go? Did something happen with Jerome?"

She looked away. "No, I…I just need to be alone right now."

Ed put his hands on her shoulders. "Come on, I feel your pain. If Jerome did something—"

Ann shook her head. "No, he didn't. It's me, not him." She pulled away and slumped to the ground. She pulled her knees up to her chest and buried her face in her hands. "Please go."

Ed knelt, placing a hand on her knee. "Hey, it's just me. If you don't want to talk, okay, but I'm staying." He didn't mention just being near her seemed to settle both the beast and the strange rage he kept feeling.

"It didn't work," she muttered after a few moments.

Ed, where are you? Jax demanded. *We've been looking everywhere for you.*

He'd almost forgotten about them after blocking out their calls.

Wolfy? Ceara yelled.

I'm with Ann. Everything is fine, he told them. *Go get some sleep.*

Did you attack Jerome? Ceara wanted to know. *Did you stop him and Ann from—?*

Ann can hear you, she snapped.

Ed bit back a chuckle. *So much for mind links being private. No, I didn't attack anyone,* Ed replied. *Stop calling me. I'm in control.*

So, how far did you and Jerome get? Ceara asked with a giggle.

Ed slammed up a mental wall, silencing Jax and Ceara's voices.

"Sorry about that," he added. "What do you mean it didn't work?"

"The circle." Ann sniffed. "It didn't work. I did everything my father showed me today." She shook her head. "I don't understand why."

Ed slipped an arm around her, relieved when she didn't push him away. "You're not a failure," he told her. "Maybe it wasn't meant to work."

"Thanks for making me feel better," she grumbled.

"No, I mean it could be any number of reasons."

"I wanted it to work. I accept what I am now. I did everything the way Papa did."

"Maybe that's the problem."

She frowned as she looked up. "What does that mean?"

"You're not Darius." Her frown turned into a glare. "I mean you're you, not him. Maybe your magic works differently from his." Ed took her hand, pulled to her feet. "Come on." He wrapped an arm around her as he picked her up.

"What—?" Ann began.

Ed blurred, reappearing in the centre of the stones. "Try again." He set her back on her feet.

"Ed, I don't want to be here."

"Try. You've spent months telling me I can control my beast. Now it's my turn to return the favour."

Ann heaved a sigh and muttered words of power again.

Around them the stones flashed. "See." She dropped her arms to her sides in exasperation. "Now will you let me go back to the grove?"

"It did work. Maybe you're not trying hard enough."

Ann's eyes flashed with power. "Ed —"

He came up behind her, slipping an arm around her waist. "Close your eyes and focus. Just like you used to when we practiced magic as kids."

Ann sighed again, then squeezed her eyes shut. Her heart thudded in his ears.

"Focus on what you want. The power of the stones," he whispered. "They are yours to command."

Energy hummed and vibrated around them like instruments vibrating with sound. His beast clawed for control again. He flinched but pushed it away. He couldn't risk breaking Ann's concentration.

Ann said the words to the spell. The stones glowed brighter. Ed sensed it wouldn't be enough.

He put his other arm around her as his hands flared with light. For a moment, he thought it was Ann's magic. *No, not hers. Mine,* he realised. *I still have magic.* Ed almost laughed with joy. *Guess I didn't lose it after all.*

He sensed Ann's power, too. Raw, untapped power, deep inside her. He wondered if she knew how much she had.

Ann glanced up at him, her eyes alight with golden light. She said something else and gripped his hands. His magic intertwined with hers as if they were one.

She'd said words of power—different words.

The ground beneath their feet trembled and groaned. Ed pulled her tighter to his chest.

It's alright. He felt, more than heard, her words.

Lightning flashed as the tremors became more violent. The earth groaned and moved as a giant bluestone rose and stood erect. One by one, more stones appeared. Lightning danced around the stone ring as their magic combined. The bolts of lightning jumped from one stone to another, fusing the stones together. Another stone shot up, flying overhead. It landed on top of the other standing stones, linking together two sentinel stones.

Once complete, blue light pulsed and vibrated within the circle then expanded outward, enveloping everything in its path. The standing stone circle was complete for the first time in thousands of years.

Ann laughed and wrapped her arms around him. "I did it. *We* did it."

He laughed, picking her up and swinging her around. "See? You just needed to find your way."

"You still have magic. I felt it."

Still reeling from the power and happiness, he bent. For a moment their eyes locked, their faces only inches apart.

In one move, he could kiss her, taste her as he'd wanted to do for a long time.

To Ed's surprise, Ann didn't pull back. She reached up and touched his cheek.

Ed pulled back. All at once, the magic around them faded. The stones darkened and fell silent.

Ann sagged against him.

Ed stumbled as he caught hold of her. His energy was gone, too. Slumping back onto the ground, he wrapped his arms tight around her, and let sleep drag him under.

Ed blinked as he awakened. Bright sunlight dazzled him. Ann still lay snuggled up in his arms. Power hummed from the stones and he snuggled closer to Ann. A shadow fell over as the sun faded as something big blocked it out. A roar filled the air, and the ground shook. Ed bolted up and saw the wyvern flying overhead. Blue light radiated from the stones. He heard shouts in the distance, and spotted Jerome and the other druids firing arrows.

"Ann?" He shook her shoulder. "Ann, wake up."

Ceara came running over. "Here you are. We've been looking everywhere for you two," She puffed. "There is a dragon."

"I see that." Ed rose to his feet.

Ann groaned as she came awake. "What's going on?"

"Come on, wake up, lovebirds. Look, dragon!" Ceara cried.

A crow squawked as it flew over to them. It shifted into Jax.

"Dragon?" Ann scrambled up and looked skyward.

"It's the wyvern I met last night," Ed remarked.

"How can you meet a dragon?" Ceara asked, pulling out her shock rods.

"Wyvern," he corrected.

The wyvern circled. The light from the stones continued to shield them within the circle.

"Ann, tell them to stop shooting at it," Ed snapped.

"Are you mad?" Jax drew his staff, readying himself for attack.

"No, it's hasn't attacked yet, has it?" Ed knew he couldn't let them or the druids harm it. He felt a connection to it he didn't understand.

Maybe it was a kinship, since he often felt trapped with a beast inside his body.

"It's a dragon; I doubt it's here to make friends with us," Ceara said.

Ed blurred away, moving from the protection of the stones' shield. Ann called after him, but he didn't answer.

He stopped when he reached the grove. The wyvern swooped down, landing a few feet away.

Ed approached with caution. "Why have you come here?" Although careful, he didn't sense a threat from it. Nor did his beast seem bothered by it.

Ann, Ceara, and Jax reappeared beside him in a flash of blue orbs.

"Ed, what are you doing?" Ann asked.

"Losing his mind, by the looks of it," Ceara remarked. "Ed—"

He held up a hand to silence them. "Shush, let's see what it wants."

"Brother, it's a *dragon*," Jax protested.

The huge beast roared. Ed's own eyes flashed from amber to emerald. He reached out and touched the wyvern's head.

The wyvern roared again, tossing its head from side to side.

"Ann, don't," he said as she raised her hands. "It's not here to hurt us."

"Then why is it here?" Ceara asked, keeping her shock rod out just as Jax did with his staff.

Ed closed his eyes. The wailing rang through his ears again, but this time, it didn't hurt so much.

His heart ached as he sensed the wyvern's distress. "It doesn't want to be here, but it's been ordered to attack."

"Since when do you communicate with dragons?" Jax asked.

"I'm not. I feel its emotions on some level." He shook his head. "I can't explain it."

"I don't feel anything," Ceara pointed out. "What does it want?"

"It came to deliver a message." His brow creased.

The wyvern opened its mouth and dropped a crystal to the ground.

Jax bent and picked it up, scanning it for energy. He also had some control over stone magic.

"I don't sense—" Jax yelped, dropping the crystal as it flared with heat

A hologram appeared, and a smiling Urien stared back at them. "Hello, sister," he said. "Well done for raising the shield at Trewa. Didn't know you had it in you."

Ann's eyes narrowed. "What do you want?" she demanded. "And where in Erthea did you get a wyvern from?"

Urien laughed. "That's not important, but there are plenty more from where they came from. I want to invite you all to the palace. We need to talk."

"What makes you think she'll do that?" Ceara sneered.

"If you don't, every leader from around the five lands will die. I'll order my wyverns to attack and kill every druid in Trewa." Urien's smile faded. "Your shield won't hold forever. Not under the strength of dragon fire. Be here tonight, or I'll attack." The image winked out before any of them could say another word.

The wyvern let out a mournful wail as it stared at them with tears that glistened in the sunlight. Then it turned and took to the sky. Within moments, it vanished over the horizon.

CHAPTER 20

"Wait, you want to walk right into Urien's hands?" Ed demanded, staring at Ann open-mouthed.

They all stood in her cabin, having gone there after Urien's little wakeup call. Urien had used one of her father's devices to send out a call to all leaders of the five lands, demanding they come to the palace at once. She had no idea how Urien would have found the device, but what was done was done. Now she had to act.

"I have to get to that meeting. Urien must be planning to do something big to have used the device at all." Ann paused and bit her lip. "Ceara can get me in there by taking me in as a prisoner. It would be safer if you and Jax didn't come with us."

Ed's mouth fell open. "What? No. No way. I'm not letting—"

"You can't be serious," Jax remarked. "I knew that bloody Gliss would turn on you."

"I'm the one who suggested it to her," Ann said. "There's no point in arguing. We're going. You and Ed can sneak in along with the rest of the leaders."

Ed shook his head. "No, I'm not letting you put yourself at risk—"

Her eyes narrowed. "Since when do you *let* me do anything?" she demanded. "This is my choice. I can't take the two of you with me; Urien would never believe Ceara overpowered all three of us. It's better if I go. I'm the one Urien wants."

"Could you please not talk about me as if I weren't in the room?" Ceara scowled. "Do you have a better way of getting there? I'm the only one who can get in and out without raising suspicion."

"No, but there are much less dangerous ways of doing it." Ed crossed his arms and turned to Ceara. "You've said yourself that Urien doesn't trust you anymore."

"Bringing Ann to him is the perfect way to prove my loyalty. It will make him think I want him back—which I don't, by the way." She shuddered. "So unless you have a better way of us getting in without bloodshed, I'm all ears."

Ed's jaw tightened and he muttered an oath under his breath.

"I have to get in there before Urien has the chance to wipe out most of the leaders of the five lands," Ann said. "Ceara can get me in there. He'll keep sending more Gliss after us if I stay here and do nothing. I think our time here has ended. I don't want to put the druids at any more risk."

"You haven't even perfected your spell yet," Ed protested. "What are you going to do if you do confront Urien?"

"The only way of knowing if the spell works is to try it." She rolled up her cloak and shoved it into her pack. "Pack up your things and say your goodbyes. Ceara and I are leaving." She had no idea what she was going to say to her uncle yet.

To her surprise, Blaise came in. "I agree with Ed and Jax. It's too dangerous for you to go with only a Gliss by your side." He glared at Ceara.

She turned and scowled at Edward. "I can't believe you called my uncle for help."

Ed raised his chin. "Maybe he can make you see sense."

She turned her attention back to Blaise. "Since when do you care about what happened to me?" Ann raised an eyebrow.

"We're still family. Just because you can't die doesn't make you invincible. Darius' magic isn't infallible. Urien could still find a way to undo it, which means your death could become permanent." Blaise put his hands on her shoulders. "I'd rather not lose what little family I do have left. You're welcome to stay here among your people. The power of the stones will keep Urien at bay for now."

Ann shook her head. "No, staying here only puts all of you at risk. I couldn't live with myself if more people died because of me," she said. "No, it's best if we leave. I was foolish to think I could stay here. Ceara and I are going to Larenth. End of discussion."

"You can't go running in there blind," Ed snapped. "How will you get out? Have you even thought this plan through?"

"I can send the four of you to the outskirts of the palace," Blaise said. All four of them gaped at him.

Ann frowned at her uncle. "How?"

"Your father had a secret way in and out only he and I knew about."

That seemed impossible. Ann thought she'd known every inch of the palace and its grounds. "Where is it?"

"It's a small gazebo on the outskirts of the grounds. You and Xander used to play there as children," Blaise explained. "Your father made it as a portal to transport in and out—we designed it together. It looks nothing like a portal. All its inner workings are concealed. We made in case he ever needed to escape without leaving any trace of his own magic behind."

"Urien will sense her the minute she arrives," Ed pointed out.

Blaise shook his head. "No, he won't—not unless she uses magic herself. The portal is designed to be undetectable. It will get you there."

"Can we use it as a way out again?" Ann asked. She'd planned as far as getting in but hadn't got as far as getting out. She figured they would find a way out once they got there, just as they had last time they'd faced Urien.

"Yes, but you'll need this." Blaise pulled out a pendant with a white oak tree carved into black stone, surrounded by three stars. The symbol of the archdruid. "This belonged to your father." Blaise held it out to her. "Never let it out of your sight."

She remembered Darius wearing it all the time. "I thought he still had it on him the night he died." Her fingers wrapped around the stone. It felt cool to her touch, and a lump rose in her throat.

"He sent it to me the night he was killed." Blaise wrapped his hands over hers. "I don't want you to go but I know nothing I say will stop you. You are the archdruid. Embrace it. You'll need all your strength to defeat Urien."

Ann wrapped her arms around him. "Thank you." She sniffed. "Be ready," she said to the others. "We're leaving for the palace within the hour. After that, we're not coming back to Trewa."

"Let's hope we're still alive long enough to go somewhere else," Jax muttered.

"Where are we going to next?" Ceara asked. "Something tells me I won't be seeing a soft bed for quite a while."

"We'll cross that bridge when we come to it," Ed said. "There are a lot of different places to hide within Caselhelm. We'll find somewhere to stay for a little while, then move on. Better get used to life as this a fugitive, little sister."

Ann left the house to go and say goodbye to Sage. The druid hugged her and told her to be safe.

"Are you sure you'll be alright here?" Ann asked her.

Sage smiled. "There's life in these old bones yet." She hugged Ann tight. "The path of the archdruid can be a lonely one. I'm glad you have Jax and Edward with you."

232

"And Ceara," Ann added. "I know you may not believe it, but she has changed. I hope you can find in your heart to forgive her someday."

"Be safe. You and I may have our differences, but you are family to me."

"You be safe, too." Ann returned her embrace.

As she left Sage's house, she headed out to find Jerome outside his hut. She hesitated when she saw him. After the disaster of last night and falling asleep with Ed again, she didn't know what to say.

"Rhiannon."

Ann winced. Why did he have to call her that? "Hey, I came to say goodbye." Best to get it over with than draw it out any longer.

Jerome frowned. "You're leaving? Why? You are the—you belong here with your people."

"I think we both know I'm not like other archdruids. I'm more of a rogue. But I'm glad we got to see each other again. I wish we could've spent—"

Jerome cupped her face and kissed her. "We'll see each other again. I know it."

She pulled away and tucked a lock of hair behind her ear. "Maybe." Ann didn't know what else to say. "Listen, about last night—"

Ann turned around to see Ed standing behind her with a pained expression on his face. "We're ready to leave," he said and turned away from her.

Ann felt a pang of guilt and hurried after him to go back into Blaise's house.

Blaise led them to the back garden. Outside stood a small metal gazebo. It was an octagonal building with turrets on top. Ann remembered seeing one like this back at the palace. It had been used as a place to sit and tell stories during the summer months when she was a child. She, Ed, and the others all tried to outmatch each other with different stories.

"All four of you need to be careful. Once you're there, I will destroy this part of the portal so none of you can return. I won't risk Urien finding a way back here," Blaise warned. "I can't help you once you're there."

"We understand. I've been alone for the past five years. Try not to worry so much." Ann hugged him one last time.

Blaise glanced at Ed and Jax. "Thank you both for helping keep my family safe." He flicked a glance toward Ceara. "I hope you're as trustworthy as my niece thinks you are."

"I am on her side. Believe that." Ceara stomped inside the gazebo.

"Be careful." Blaise squeezed Ann's shoulder. "Don't go so long without coming to see me next time. You'll always have a place here among our people."

"Goodbye, Uncle." Ann smiled and stepped inside the gazebo.

Blaise muttered words of power. Static flashed over the metal structure.

Ann's head spun as she and the others were knocked to the floor. It felt like being sucked up into a tornado as light whirled around them. Stars danced around them as the gazebo moved through time and place, taking them away from the safety of Trewa and through the different planes of existence.

Orbs sparkled around them as their bodies and the gazebo reformed. Ann yelped as she landed on something soft.

"Argh, your uncle never mentioned how awful that would feel." Ceara groaned and clutched her head. "That feels worse than when you use magic to transport us to different places."

Jax grumbled, "I think I might have left my stomach behind."

Ann looked down, realising she now lay on top of Ed. "Sorry." Her cheeks flushed with heat.

"No problem." He tried to move, and she fell against him as she attempted to get up.

"Get off me!" Ceara gave Jax a shove.

"Oh, like I want to be touching you, woman." Jax glowered at her, then glanced over at Ann and Ed. "Not interrupting anything, are we?"

Ann felt her cheeks burn hotter and she rolled away from Edward. "Of course not." She rose and peered into the empty garden, half-expecting guards or Gliss to come running. Yet she saw no one underneath the old tree.

The gardens looked different from what she remembered. Back in her father's day, they had been well-kept. Now the flowers were all dead, the grass stood overgrown, and brambles curled and grew in every direction.

"So what's the plan?" Jax asked.

"Ceara and I get in. I'll stay until the meeting. You two will bust in and get everyone out safely," Ann replied. "The meeting is scheduled for today."

"I still think Urien will be suspicious," Ed added. "Maybe if I were with you, or even Jax, it would look more convincing."

"Of course he will, which is why Ceara is taking me in as a prisoner and pretending to be on his side." She brushed dust off her leathers. "For the final time, no. You and Jax aren't coming with us. Especially not you. Ceara wouldn't be able to overpower you or Jax very easily."

Ceara raised her chin. "I could if I had enough time."

Jax glared at Ceara. "How do we know this wasn't your plan all along?" he demanded.

Ceara's lip curled. "I'm never going to be on that bastard's side," she sneered. "For the love of the gods, I thought you trusted me now?"

"We do." Ed nodded. "I'd still be happy if we didn't have to split up."

"I'll call you when I need you. The main thing for you to do is to get the other leaders to safety," Ann told the others. "Then I can finally try out my spell to save Xander." She'd spent weeks trying to get it right, but the only real way to test it was on Urien himself.

"We shouldn't be out in the open like this," Ed remarked. "We should head to the old Black quarters like we did last time we were here. Jax and I can hide out there."

"No, that's too obvious. Urien will suspect you and Jax will have followed her," Ceara said. "Especially you. You never leave her side."

"Told you we hadn't thought this plan through," Jax grumbled.

Ann ignored their bickering and clutched her father's pendant as she moved outside. *"Remember you are the archdruid,"* Darius's voice echoed through her mind. *"This is a key, and the symbol of the power we possess."*

She saw the door she'd seen on the other side and muttered, *"Reveala."*

Light flashed as a wooden door appeared.

"Ann, you can't use magic out in the open like this," Ed hissed as he peered beside her.

Ceara frowned. "What's that door? Why is it standing in the middle of nowhere like that?"

"It must be the vault Ann's been looking for," Jax remarked as he and Ceara moved outside of the gazebo.

"It's not my magic; it's my father's." She reached out but found no visible handle.

The door creaked open. "Hurry, get inside." Ann motioned for them to go in.

Ed went through first, followed by Jax and Ceara. The runes around the door frame flared and crackled with power.

Ann glanced back to make sure no one else was around then stepped through the door.

Light blurred around her as Ann reappeared in another room with a high vaulted ceiling. The walls were dark and shimmered with runes. When she reached out, power crackled against her fingers as the walls flickered in and out of existence. Whatever this place was, it didn't seem to exist on their plane of existence. Perhaps not even on Erthea at all. This was something else, something that existed beyond time and place.

Jax, Ceara, and Ed all lay sprawled on the floor.

Ed appeared to be the only one conscious as he scrambled up into a sitting position.

"What happened?" Ann gasped. "Are you alright?"

Ed groaned, rubbed the back of his neck. "I guess your father didn't invite people in here. Something knocked us out—or rather, knocked them out." He motioned to Jax and Ceara. "Maybe my beast side is good for something."

Ann knelt to check on the others and touched their throats. "They're still breathing. I guess I should've come through first. I think they'll be okay. Their pulses are strong." She moved over to him and touched his forehead. "Are you sure you're alright?"

"I'm fine." He scrambled up and shrugged off her touch. Having him push her away like that stung.

"What's wrong?" Ann noticed he seemed a little distant since he'd seen her kiss Jerome. She couldn't understand why, though. She might not even see Jerome again. "Listen, about earlier when Jerome kissed—"

"Ow." Ceara clutched at her head. "What just hit me? I feel like I have the world's worst hangover." She pushed her long black hair off her face. "Did one of you use magic on me?"

"Must've been a ward," Ann replied. "My father would have spelled this place to prevent anyone else from being able to access it."

"Magic isn't supposed to affect me like that," the Gliss grumbled.

Jax sprang up, staff drawn. "Did you just attack me?" He glared at Ceara.

"If I had, you'd know it." She scowled back at him. "And no, I didn't. I don't have the power to knock you unconscious like that."

Ed frowned, glancing around the strange passageway. "Is this the vault?" he asked. "How did you find it?"

Ann shook her head. "I didn't. I just saw it after we first arrived. The door was just sitting there, plain as day." She shrugged and touched the crest at her throat. "This must be the key to seeing and accessing the vault. I wonder if Blaise knew he had it all along." Perhaps he'd waited until he thought he could trust her before giving her the crest. Either way, it didn't matter. She'd finally found it.

The four of them moved down the passageway and into a much larger room. Shelves reached from floor to ceiling were covered in books, crystals, stones and weapons. The walls appeared to be whitewashed stone. A tapestry depicting Trin and another showing the great stones of Trewa lined the other side of the room. Two divans stuffed with cushions sat in the centre of the room along with a large table surrounded by four chairs. Strange, she hadn't expected the vault to look so homey.

"This is it." She nodded. "It could take decades get through all this."

"We'll find something." Ed touched her shoulder and gave a squeeze.

"Now we're safe, let's get to work on planning our way in and way out of the palace."

CHAPTER 21

Ann's stomach fluttered with nerves as Ceara led her across the grounds. They'd even found some shackles in the vault to make it look realistic. Ed and Jax still hadn't been happy about the idea. She knew this to be the easiest way to get in. She asked Ceara to make things look even more realistic by hitting her, and now sported a black eye and a bloodied lip.

"Relax. You're even more nervous than I am," Ann remarked, trying to ignore the metal digging into her wrists.

"Urien has a hold on me. I don't want to go near him, but…" Ceara's voice trailed off.

"Just remember you're stronger than him." Ann smiled. "I don't have doubts about you, so don't have any about yourself."

Ceara nodded. "Right." She paused. "Why do you believe in me so much?"

"Everyone deserves a second chance."

"Thanks, you're a good…friend. More than I deserve." Ceara averted her gaze.

"Come on, let's go."

Ceara tugged on the shackles as they headed for the doors. Three guards stood there, wearing black uniforms. They were different from the uniforms of the old Black Guard; they wore black tunics underneath their armour. The Black had worn leather cloaks.

Ann resisted the urge to wince. Was Urien trying to recreate their father's Guard? If so, why? Urien had thought Darius's elite guard was useless, but then again, she had no idea what went through her brother's mind these days. If he wanted to pass himself off as the archdruid, maybe creating a new Black was a way of doing that for him.

"Let me pass. I'm here to take the archdruid to Urien," Ceara said.

The lead guard, a dark-haired man with dark eyes, stepped forward, one hand on the hilt of his sword. "This is the archdruid?" He eyed Ann and peered at her, his face only inches from hers. She resisted the urge to wince from the foul stench of ale on his breath.

"Don't you see the Valeran crest on her? The symbol of the archdruid?" Ceara slapped him. "Don't question a Gliss. Just let me through." She tugged on Ann's shackles, pulling her closer. "I'm not standing around here all day."

"We have orders not to let—"

Ceara kept hold of Ann's shackles in one hand and pulled out her rod with the other, jamming it into the guard's neck. He fell to his knees, screaming. She kicked him in the head, and he slumped to the ground. "Who wants to go next?"

The second guard yanked the door open, and the third moved aside.

Ceara led Ann through and down the hall, past more guards. The entry hall looked more or less as Ann remembered. The rich tapestries that had once hung there had vanished, along with the gleaming suits of armour that her father had been so fond of. Now the walls appeared barren. Almost as though the palace too had died along with her parents. Ann tried to move her mind away from the past. What good would remembering what the palace had looked like even do? This wasn't her home. That had been a long time ago. Another lifetime. She wasn't that person anymore, but she might have to be Rhiannon Valeran again, at least for a while when she faced Urien.

Ceara dragged her through the great oak double doors and into the great hall. This room appeared unchanged in some ways. The high vaulted ceiling gleamed overhead. The beautiful white marble floor inlaid with a silver Valeran crest had turned dirty and scuffed with age. Back in her father's day, it had always gleamed, no matter how many people walked upon it.

No banners hung from the walls as they once had. The Valeran banner that had once hung from the balcony had vanished too. Her heart twisted just being back in this room. She had so many memories of being here with her father, of parties and meeting different people. People from around the five lands, even outside Almara, had graced this hall when they had come to meet her father. This had been a happy place once, full of joy and laughter. Now it felt hollow, dark, and empty. A shell of what it had once been.

Another blond-haired Gliss appeared and blocked their path. "Ceara, you're alive," she remarked. "What are you doing? I'm surprised you even came back. Some of us thought you drowned when Trin disappeared."

"I told Urien he'd regret choosing Constance over at me. I've come to prove I'm better." She yanked Ann forward. "I caught the archdruid single-handed. Now let me pass. My business is with Urien, not you."

The other Gliss's eyes narrowed. "Why should I let you anywhere near him? You threatened his life."

"Hurry up, will you?" Ann snapped. "I'm the archdruid. I shouldn't be dragged around like this. I'm sure my brother will be eager to see me."

Ceara hit her on the head. Ann winced at the pain. She'd told Ceara to treat her as if she were any other prisoner. *Guess I've only got myself to blame for that one.*

"Move, Olivia," Ceara hissed at the other Gliss. "Get out of my way, or I swear I'll kill you. I'm in no mood for dallying."

The other Gliss moved aside. "We'll see." She made a move to grab Ann's shackles.

"No, the archdruid stays with me." Ceara shoved the other Gliss aside and continued moving across the floor.

Urien sat on their father's seat up on the dais—the seat of the archdruid—and his eyes widened as his gaze fixed on them. "Ceara, I'm surprised to see you. I felt sure my spell would have finished you off by now."

Ann's stomach lurched at seeing him on their father's throne. *Her* throne.

"As you can see, I am very much alive." Ceara raised her chin. "I've brought your sister back."

Urien rose and walked down the steps of the dais. He caught hold of Ann's hair, his gaze roaming over her. "How? My sister isn't stupid."

Ann jerked her head away from him. "Unshackle me," she spat. "I am—"

"The shackles bind her magic," Ceara interrupted. "She's not a threat. She can't hurt anyone."

Constance appeared and moved out from behind the dais. "What made you come back?" She narrowed her eyes and crossed her arms. "I thought you would have had the sense to stay away. You know you'll be punished for your betrayal, and for trying to escape."

"I've been loyal to you for years," Ceara said, ignoring the other Gliss. "I want to come back and be your favourite again. Constance is doing a lousy job. She couldn't even keep hold of Trin, could she?

"You also vowed to make me pay," Urien remarked.

"I was angry; forgive me. You know I'd never turn on you, my love." Ceara gave him a sickly-sweet smile.

"Oh, please," Ann scoffed. "I don't need to see this."

Ceara jabbed her rod against Ann's back. She sank to her knees as pain radiated down her spine. The volts of electricity shot through every nerve ending. She gritted her teeth to keep from screaming. Her legs went numb and she couldn't get back up.

"As you can see, she's no threat to anyone." Ceara smirked. "I can keep her in line."

"How did you even get her here?" Urien asked. "My spell tracked you to Trewa."

"She and I were friends once. It wasn't hard to play on that and gain her trust." Urien made a move to take the shackles from her. "Ah-ah. I won't just hand her over. I have conditions."

"What conditions?" Urien demanded, eyes narrowing.

"First of all, I want her gone." She jerked her finger toward Constance. The other Gliss glared back, her hand going to one of her shock rods. "I want to be your chief Gliss again, with all the favours that come with it."

"You dare make demands of me?" Urien's eyes darkened.

It made Ann's gut twist seeing Xander's face staring back at her. It might still look like Xander, but she could see Urien staring out through his eyes.

"If you want to keep your sister powerless, yes, I do," Ceara snapped. "I've been loyal to you for years. I deserve to lead again." She gripped Ann's shackles tighter. "Besides, I did something none of your other Gliss could do. I subdued your sister, just as you wanted. Don't I deserve some reward for that?"

"We'll see."

"My lord, you can't be serious," Constance protested. "She vowed to make you pay for discarding her. How do we know this isn't a trap?"

"Leave us. All of you," Urien ordered.

"I'm not leaving." Ceara raised her chin.

Urien's expression darkened. "I'll have you forcibly removed if I must," he hissed.

Ann gave Ceara a nudge. *Go,* she said. *Don't make a scene. I'll be alright.*

But this wasn't the plan, Ceara said. *What if I can't get to you again? How are we going to get out of here?*

Shush, don't speak to me unless you have to. I don't want to risk Urien overhearing us. Ann gave her a hard look.

Ceara reluctantly let go of her and left. Ann hoped she kept her temper under control and didn't start any fights with any of the other Gliss.

"I'm surprised you'd let one Gliss get the better of you, sister." Urien smirked as he circled round her.

Her jaw tightened. "Ceara can be a convincing little bitch when she wants to be." She held up her shackled wrists. "These aren't necessary, are they? We both know I can't hurt you without hurting Xander too."

"True, but I can't have you using any magic to stop me or my people." He gave her a hard look. "Did Ceara really capture you?"

"I would think that was obvious." She motioned to her bloodied lip and a black eye. "I wouldn't have just handed myself over to her, would I?"

"I know you better than you think, Rhiannon. You can be very persuasive in turning people to your side," he said. "And I know Ceara won't take lightly to being cast aside. You've come to stop the meeting of the leaders, haven't you?" His smile widened. "I thought you might hear the call. You'll try to save them."

Damn right, I will.

"How did you even find the device to call the leaders here?"

Urien laughed. "You're not the only one who knew of father's secrets, sister. I know where he kept his secret chambers and whatever he didn't want people to find."

"You couldn't access Papa's vault, though, could you?" She bit back a smile as Urien's eyes widened. "Yes, brother. I know you've been looking for it, too. No doubt so you can find a way to undo the spell that binds us together and protects us from death in there." She rubbed her wrists as the metal cut into them. "Why are you calling together the leaders? You don't negotiate, you take what you want and damn the consequences."

"You're right, I don't negotiate. It will be good to have you here by my side. It will prove to everyone I can conquer anyone—even the archdruid herself. Whatever you think you're going to do, you won't. I'll stop you."

"We'll see, brother. We'll see."

Ann got shoved into what had been her former bedroom. It looked more or less just as she'd left it. Same fourposter bed, same furniture. Her jewels and weapons had all vanished, yet some of her clothes still hung in the wardrobe. Why would they hang onto her clothes? Had Urien expected her to come back?

"Get dressed," Constance ordered. "Urien wants you to look presentable in front of the other leaders."

"Being forced to stay here is one thing, but I don't have to do anything you tell me to do." She crossed her arms.

Constant pulled out her rod. "I'll strip and dress you myself I have to." She smirked. "I'd enjoy nothing more than to see you on your knees begging for mercy."

Ann snorted. "I've never begged for anything. Enjoy your power whilst it lasts. Urien will soon cast you aside and have a new favourite."

"You know nothing." Constance's hand went to one of her shock rods as she took a step toward Ann.

"Urien won't want me looking battered and bruised, will he? That won't make him look good in front of the other leaders."

"Be ready in ten minutes, or I'll drag you there naked if I have to." Constance stormed out of the room.

Ann sighed and stared at the beautiful gowns she'd once worn as the archdruid's daughter. *Now I'm the archdruid and my former home is my prison.* She pulled a couple of dresses out. Unlacing her leather bodice and trousers, she pulled a white dress on, tucking the Valeran crest underneath it.

She still had the cuffs on, even if they weren't shackled together now. Constance had been nice enough to break the chains apart and thought the power of the cuffs would still work. *Good thing these cuffs don't bind my powers.*

Pulling a panel out from the wardrobe, she opened a wooden box and got to work casting a spell. Smoke filled the air as she shoved the box away and brushed her hair off her face. An image of her old self—of Rhiannon Valeran—stared back at her in the mirror. Yet this Rhiannon had an edge to her eyes. She sighed again. The old Rhiannon had died the night her parents had been killed. After she'd been forced to go into hiding, accused of a crime she didn't commit.

She wasn't Rhiannon, the druid's daughter anymore. She was Ann, the rogue archdruid. Time everyone knew the truth.

If Urien thought he could force her into submission, he'd be damn wrong. She applied make-up to her face when Urien stormed in. "What is taking so bloody long?" he demanded.

"I thought you wanted me to look presentable," she remarked. "Can't go in there with a bruised face, now can I?"

He grabbed her wrist and pulled her to her feet. "Let's go. The meeting is about to begin."

Urien pulled her down the hall past several guards until they reached the balcony that looked down into the great hall.

Below, a dozen leaders, along with their servants and guards, stood around waiting.

Ann's breath hitched. Would her spell be enough to protect them all?

CHAPTER 22

Ed fumbled with his uncomfortable clothes as they headed out onto the main road that led to Larenth Palace. He hated disguising himself, but it was the only way to get into the palace undetected. He now wore a dark, rough linen shirt, black trousers, and an old pair of boots. It made him miss his usual ranger clothing. He kept his long hair tied up at the nape of his neck.

"Look at me," Jax complained. "I'm dressed like a farmer in trousers that only reach my knees. I look like a bloody idiot!"

Ed bit back a laugh. Jax's trousers were indeed too short and only fell to knee length. His shirt didn't look much better, but Ann hadn't had much to choose from in her collection of clothing—at least not anything that would fit Jax. They were supposed to be blending in, but Jax wouldn't stand out in his ridiculous outfit. It wasn't uncommon for servants and the poor to wear ill-fitting clothing.

"You have good knees." Ed smirked. "We're lucky Ann keeps extra clothes in her bag. It makes it much easier for us to get in and out." He still didn't like the thought of Ann going off on her own with Ceara. Although he had come to trust the Gliss again, he hated the thought of not being there if something went wrong.

Jax scowled. "Where does she get all these clothes? I haven't seen her with anyone. Did she pick up a lot of different men during your time on the run?"

Ed's smile faded as he remembered seeing her kissing Jerome. He pushed that thought away. It didn't matter, especially not now.

"Why couldn't Ann make you dress like the village idiot?" Jax grumbled. "How come all of her male clothing seems to fit you?"

He shrugged. "We've moved around a lot over the past few years. We picked up different clothes along the way." He chuckled. "Stop complaining. We need to blend in."

"I'm never gonna blend in looking like this. I would have preferred to have been shackled and tortured by a Gliss than look like this." Jax tried to pull the ill-fitting trousers down over his knees.

"Careful, you might get your wish."

They followed the crowd, trying to mingle and look inconspicuous. The road was a well-worn dirt track surrounded by heavy trees on either side. The great palace loomed like a white jewel glistening on the landscape. It rose, surrounded by trees as it perched on the cliffside. Its great towers loomed like silent sentinels reaching the heavens. The blue tiles covering the roof glistened like sapphires. Its tiny windows were like a thousand eyes looking down, watching them. Great trees reached up, trying to match the palace in height and splendour.

This sight had once been so familiar to him, yet it felt strange being back here. He'd called this place home for most of his life.

Other people travelled along the road, some riding horses, others sitting on wagons or passing by in great carriages. The palace road hadn't been this busy since Darius' time. Whatever Urien had planned, it couldn't be good. He and Jax had to get inside to make sure Ann and Ceara stayed safe, no matter what.

Ed recognised some of the leaders. Many of them had come here during Darius' reign. He hoped no one recognised him or Jax from their days as Ann's bodyguards. They couldn't risk activating their glamours, as Urien would have enchantments against such things.

The beast clawed at the cage of his mind, restless and uneasy. It didn't like being apart from Ann. Ed couldn't blame it. He didn't like it either.

"You think Ceara will come through for us?" Jax asked, dodging out of the way of a horse that nearly knocked into him.

Ed shrugged. "Ann thinks she's loyal, and she has fought with us against Urien. I think she hates Urien enough to help Ann."

"Yeah, but she also loved the guy. If big brother curls his finger, she'll go running back to him."

Maybe, maybe not. Urien had proved he didn't give a damn about anyone but himself. Somehow, Ed didn't think Ceara would go back to him now. She'd had every chance to turn against them during their stay in Trewa. She had been genuinely grief-stricken at Flora's death. He doubted Ceara would ever forgive Urien for killing their mother.

"I can't believe how many people are here," he remarked. "I'm surprised they'd all come. Most of the leaders despised Orla as much as we do."

"Yeah, all lambs to the slaughter."

"I haven't seen them all come together like this since Darius was alive. Orla never managed to do it," Ed said. "Ann said Darius had a device to summon people to him. I don't want to think about what else Urien managed to get his hands on inside the palace."

"Let's hope Ann can prove she is the archdruid and stop Urien from parading himself as one."

"Urien *wants* to be the archdruid. It's why he killed Darius and Deanna."

They moved through the crowd. Several people shot glances Jax's way—much to his annoyance. Ed and Jax pushed their way through the crowd of oncoming travellers and headed straight for the gates that led inside the palace.

Two guards stood by the open gateway, both wearing black armour. It appeared different to what he and Jax had once worn during their days in the Black. The first guard was a man with long black hair and dark eyes, the other blond and blue-eyed.

Ed gave the guards a nod and waited as they approached. "Where are your papers?" the dark-haired man barked. "All guests must show identification and be checked for weapons."

Ah, no. He'd expected to be checked for weapons, but not identification. He glanced at Jax who had turned his staff into a walking stick.

"We're just humble servants." Ed bowed his head. "We have—"

A pretty redheaded woman pushed through the crowd. With her emerald eyes and low-cut bodice, she turned a few heads.

Ed stared at her and the beast perked up, excitement rushing through him. *Kin,* it whispered.

Kin? What does that mean? He averted his gaze to the ground. Servants weren't supposed to look at their superiors, and he didn't want to attract anymore unwanted attention.

"They're with me," she said in a low, sultry voice.

"And you are?" The dark-haired guard's eyes gleamed with lust.

"Lord Urien is expecting me." She handed over a roll of parchment.

The guard examined it his eyes narrowed. "Why don't they have identification?"

The woman rolled her eyes and put her hand on her hip. "They're servants; they can't even read," she scoffed. "Why would they need to? They're here to serve our needs."

The guards chuckled and nodded in agreement. They checked Ed and Jax over for weapons then finally let them pass.

The woman sauntered past the guards with Ed and Jax trailing behind her.

"Phew, that was close," Jax muttered. *Who is this woman, and why did she just help us?* He asked in thought. *Why do you look so flustered?*

Ed took hold of the woman's arm, and a jolt of recognition shot through him. "Have we met before? You seem familiar." He couldn't place her face.

Her lips curved into a smile. "Perhaps. My name is Jessa. And you are?"

"Why did you help us?" Jax frowned. "What are you after?"

Her smile widened. "You're welcome. I only helped you because I could see they wouldn't let you pass without you producing the necessary identification."

Jax's own eyes narrowed and he turned to Ed. "Do you—?" The woman vanished in a blur. One second, she had been there, the next, gone. "Where did she go?" His frown deepened. "Did she just blur like you do?"

Ed shook his head. "I don't know. She just vanished."

"What is with you acting so strange around her?" Jax asked. "I've never seen you act that strange around a woman before...Well, except a certain blond one we all know and love." He bit back a smile.

"I don't know. I felt like I knew her from somewhere." He shrugged and shook his head. Ed couldn't explain the strange feeling he'd felt toward the stranger. Some part of him had been drawn to her in a way he'd never experienced before.

"Yeah, well, let's get this over with."

They headed down the corridor, only to be confronted by two Gliss as they approached the Great Hall.

Not again. Ed glanced around for any sign of the redhead. No such luck this time.

"What are you two doing loitering in the hall?" the blond haired Gliss asked. Her hand went to one of her shock rods.

Ed suppressed a shudder, and the beast began to claw at the edge of his mind again. It wanted control. It wanted to get out, but he knew that was the last thing he could afford to do whilst here. He had to act normal, like a human. No one could know what he really was.

"We are looking for our mistress," Ed blurted out. "We can't seem to find her, and we got lost."

The other Gliss, a raven-haired woman, narrowed her eyes at them. "A likely story. Show us your identification papers. No one gets in or out without them."

Ah, what is it with them and papers? Papers could easily be forged, and they would be easy enough to come by in certain parts of the five lands.

Ed spotted something in his belt, a rolled-up piece of parchment. Strange, he hadn't noticed that earlier. Had the woman slipped it on him before she disappeared? He pulled it out and handed it to the Gliss.

The blond Gliss snatched it, then unrolled it. Her eyes narrowed as she examined the scroll's contents.

After a moment's hesitation, she shoved the scroll back into his hand and waved them through.

That was close, Jax said as they followed the crowd of people toward the great hall. *What's on that scroll and where did it come from?*

Ed shrugged. *That woman must have given it to us. Although I can't imagine why.*

Silence descended over the crowd as Urien led Ceara out onto the dais. Ed's heart stopped when he saw her. Well, at least they knew she had made it in safely. But where was Ann?

Urien dragged her down the steps of the grand staircase. She now wore a long white robe and looked every inch the archdruid.

Ed sighed. *Thank the spirits she's alright.*

"Welcome, everyone," Urien said, taking his place on the dais. "I called you here today in an effort to bring the lands together."

Orla appeared by his side. "After five years of being banished, it's time for my son to take his true place as the—"

Someone started clapping in the background, and a figure emerged from the shadows: Darius. With his dark blond hair and piercing blue eyes, he commanded the same presence in death as he had in life. Blood covered his shirt and dripped from his mouth. "Well done for bringing all these people together, boy." He laughed.

What is that? Jax asked. *Darius died five years ago. We both saw it.*

Must be a spell. Ann must have cast an illusion spell to make Urien think it's Darius' spirit, Ed replied. *I saw Darius die. It's not him.*

Urien turned pale as all colour drained from his face. "You…you're dead," he gasped.

"You're no archdruid. Rhiannon always had my power, even before you killed me," Darius said. "You killed me and my wife. You don't deserve to sit in my seat, and you'll never take my place."

Urien raised his hand and threw a fireball at Darius. "You're dead! You're dead!" he screamed. "Why can't you stay that way? How many times do I have to kill you?"

The leaders gasped and murmured to each other.

Orla grabbed Urien's arm. "Stop, it's a trick." She glanced at Ann. "This is your doing."

Ann raised her hand, sending the demon crashing across the room as Darius vanished. "I'm the archdruid." Her eyes flashed with fire. "One way or another, I'll rip you out of Xander's body and send you straight back to where I banished you to."

Urien glowered at her. "You're supposed to be powerless."

"Yeah, well, I told you you'd regret turning on me." Ceara grabbed Constance and shoved a rod into her neck.

Urien threw a fireball at the crowd, who screamed and scattered. It bounced off a glowing shield of energy. All at once, the image of Ann faded as Urien hurled a fireball at her.

Ed grinned. *Time for the games to begin.*

CHAPTER 23

Ann watched from the balcony as her illusion spell played out. Watching Urien cower at the sight of their father made her smile. If Urien wanted to talk, fine. But she wouldn't be doing it as a prisoner.

Time he and everyone else in the five lands knew who the real archdruid was.

Ann swept down the steps, her long white gown billowing as she moved.

She muttered words of power. Magical vines twisted and wrapped themselves around Orla, trapping her in place.

"How dare you?" Orla screeched.

"Silence. You don't get to speak here," Ann snapped. Her eyes blazed with blue light as she let her power roam free.

Ann prayed her spell would be enough to protect them. If not, Ed, Jax, and Ceara would be ready.

Ann raised her hand. Urien screamed as Xander's body was blown apart in a burst of black. She stopped on the steps of the dais and waited. In a blur of black and with an anguished cry, Urien began to reform.

Ann headed up the steps. Her father's throne looked just as she remembered. The seat of the archdruid. It blazed with light at her approach, as if welcoming her.

She took a seat on the throne. If anyone doubted her claim to be the archdruid, there would be no room for doubt now. The ancient wood felt strong and powerful as she sat down. The light emanating from the throne bathed her in a white glow.

"Brother." She flashed him a smile.

Urien gasped as Xander's body became whole once more. "Sister."

"You wanted to talk, so here I am." If he thought he could drag her down in shackles, he'd have to think again. "Although I can't imagine what there is for us to discuss."

"You killed me," Urien growled.

"Oh, don't be so melodramatic, brother. I didn't kill you. I just blew you up for a moment." Her smile widened. "We can't kill each other, remember?" She flicked a glance toward the leaders. "Was it really necessary to drag all these people here?"

Urien patted himself down as if to make sure he was whole. "I need you here, and we have much to discuss."

"Still claiming to be the archdruid, I see." Ann rose and the throne blazed with power. "Papa always said lies have a way of coming out."

"Ironic, given how much he lied to us both," Urien said.

"Well, I'm here, so talk. Are you going to confess in front of everyone how you and your bitch of a mother killed our father and my mother?" Her eyes flared with power. "Or are you going to give Xander back? Because I doubt we have anything else to discuss but that."

"No, sister. I won't give up Xander unless you give me my own body back." Urien took the steps up to the dais. "As for our father, well, I doubt many in this room miss him."

Ann's grip on the throne tightened, and the throne's light blazed a fiery red.

Urien came and sat beside her, at her right hand. The place she'd once sat at her father's side.

Ann kept her face impassive. She wouldn't dare show a hint of emotion. Not around him. "What is it you want, then? If it's oblivion, I'll be glad to send you back to it."

"Come now, Rhiannon. We shouldn't be fighting. We're together again. I told you I never wanted to hurt you. We should be working together to restore the five lands, so I have a proposition for you."

She bit back a laugh. "What could you ever have to offer me?"

"Freedom, for one thing. A chance for you to no longer have to run around and hide who you are."

"Who's hiding? I've been doing my best to fight your mother for the last five years." She rested her chin on her hand as if bored.

"Don't you want people to know your innocence?" Urien asked. "You must be tired of living in the shadows. If you joined me, you wouldn't have to hide anymore."

She rolled her eyes and rose. "Why would I ever join you?"

"Because despite everything, we were family once. You, me, and Xander could be again."

Ann gritted her teeth and crossed her arms. "You killed our father right in front of me. What makes you think I could ever forgive you for that?"

"Because I want my family back. It was Father's desire to divide us. Don't let him do that. I want you and Xander here again, with me." Urien stood and moved closer to her.

Ann burst out laughing. "You don't *want* me, Urien. You *need* me," she hissed. "You need the power of the archdruid by your side. No doubt whatever power helped you and Orla take over won't help. Why don't you tell me who that was?"

Urien's jaw tightened. "You have no idea who or what you're dealing with. They're more powerful than anything you've faced before."

"You mean the elders, then?" She'd always suspected they might be involved.

He gritted his teeth. "Don't think you can take them on."

"They won't help you anymore, will they?" Ann didn't need to hear the answer to know the truth. "You should know I'd never join you."

"Do you really think you can take the elders on alone? You'll die," Urien scoffed. "The archdruid's place has always been working for them. That's the way it's always been. You can run around with your rogues, but deep down you know this is where you belong."

"I can't die, remember? Thanks to Papa's spell. Besides, I'm not alone. I have a family. One you'll never part of again." Her hands clenched into fists. "My place has never been here. Things need to change. The five lands have been in chaos long enough, I'll do everything in my power to bring about that change." She raised her hands to blast him again.

Urien raised his own hand, deflecting her magic right toward Orla.

Orla screamed as her body erupted in flames. The fire ripped her body apart. Lightning flashed and exploded. The force of the explosion reverberated around the room, making Ann and the others stumble.

Ann caught hold of the edge of her father's throne.

Urien smiled. "Thank you, sister. I've been wanting to get rid of her for weeks now. If I'm to rule, I'll never share my power with anyone. Besides, she was only a means to an end. She stood in my way, just like our father."

Ann raised her hand and began to chant the spell she'd been working on for the past few months.

Urien staggered and his eyes flashed with power. He sent a bolt of lightning toward her.

Ann dove out of the way and returned fire, sending a column of flame at him. The ground trembled as their magic clashed.

People screamed as the chandelier came crashing down, sending glass and crystal everywhere.

The Gliss started grabbing the leaders and striking them with magic.

Ed, Ceara, Jax, stop the Gliss, Ann called. *Get everyone out of here.*

What about you? Ceara asked.

I'll be fine. Go. Ann raised her hand again, blasting Urien.

Urien staggered, almost falling down the steps of the dais. "You can't kill me, Rhiannon. You couldn't kill me the night I killed our father, you can't do it now," Urien goaded. "I'm protected from death."

An image of Darius lying on the floor bleeding out flashed through her mind. Her face dropped. To the spirits with banishment. It would be too good for him.

Instead, she muttered words not to banish, but to kill, just as Urien did the same.

Light exploded, hitting them both the same time. Ann doubled over as pain reverberated through every nerve ending.

Urien cried out too. "What was that?" he gasped.

"Hello, lover." Ceara appeared and shoved a shock rod into his neck. It made him scream.

Jax shoved a knife through Urien's chest. "Sorry, Xander, but since you can't die, that's for our mum."

Ed appeared at Ann's side. "You alright?" he asked.

She nodded.

Urien raised his hand.

"Don't bother," Ed growled. "You know you can't kill each other whilst Darius' spell remains in place."

Ann moved over to Urien's side and muttered the spell again. Light flashed over Xander's body as he coughed. "Ann?" he gasped.

"Xander, is that you?" She knelt beside him.

"It's Urien trying to trick us," Ceara sneered.

"No, it's him." Ann reached out grasped his hand.

"Urien wants to gain the elders' favour again. He killed Orla to open a portal. Blood sacrifices are the only magic strong enough to break through the mists to parts of Asral and Lulrien."

"Do you know which elder helped him and Orla to kill our parents?"

"Urien's forces will be here soon. You need to get out of here. All of you."

"No." Ann chanted the spell again.

Xander gripped her wrist. "No, Papa's spell will protect us. Urien is using it too. My power will protect him," he said. "The only way to banish him is to unlink us. Now go."

Ann gripped his wrist and said the spell anyway.

Xander winced. "He's coming back. Go!" He shoved her toward Ed. "Stab me again. If I die, you'll slow him down for a few moments. It might buy you enough time to get away."

Ceara drew her knife and shoved it through his chest. "Sorry," she murmured.

Xander's eyes became glassy as his breath left his body.

"Ann." Ed gripped her hand. "We have to go."

She didn't want to go. Xander was still her little brother. She wanted to stay, to find a way to save him.

Ann pulled her hand away from Ed's and turned back toward the dais. "Like I said, brother. Things need to change." She raised her hand. Fire enveloped the archdruid's throne. It froze for a moment, sparkling with light. Then it blew apart.

She flinched as pain stabbed through her chest as her connection to the throne's power broke. The throne that had been the seat of the archdruid for over three thousand years was gone.

"Ann?" Ed said again.

She nodded and said the words for transference.

The four of them reappeared outside the palace. After making sure the leaders were alright, they left and headed through the grounds. Many people had sent curious or angry glances her way.

"Hey, doesn't this mean you've been proven innocent now?" Ceara asked. "Maybe the other leaders—"

Ann sighed. "Today won't change anything even if anyone believes I'm innocent. Most of the leaders either despised or feared my father. They won't help me." She caught hold of the metal structure. "Urien still has Caselhelm and he has someone else helping him. Some other more powerful force—I suspect whoever it has helped him and Orla to kill my parents."

Ed squeezed her shoulder. "We didn't fail. Xander helped us, and we saved all those people."

"Urien still got what he wanted, didn't he?"

"Maybe, but it also gives us a chance to explore beyond the mists, too. I have a feeling we'll both find answers there." Ann glanced back at the palace. "And maybe I'm closer to finding out who killed my father."

If you enjoyed this book please leave a review on Amazon or book site of your choice.

For updates on more books and news releases sign up for my newsletter on tiffanyshand.com/newsletter

ALSO BY TIFFANY SHAND

Rising Darkness

Excalibar Investigations Complete Box Set

SHADOW WALKER SERIES

Shadow Walker

Shadow Spy

Shadow Guardian

Shadow Walker Complete Box Set

THE AMARANTHINE CHRONICLES BOOK 1

Betrayed By Blood

Dark Revenge

The Final Battle

SHIFTER CLANS SERIES

The Alpha's Daughter

Alpha Ascending

The Alpha's Curse

The Shifter Clans Complete Box Set

TALES OF THE ITHEREAL

Fey Spy

Outcast Fey

Rogue Fey

Hunted Fey

Tales of the Ithereal Complete Box Set

THE FEY GUARDIAN SERIES

Memories Lost

Memories Awakened

Memories Found

The Fey Guardian Complete Series

THE ARKADIA SAGA

Chosen Avatar

Captive Avatar

Fallen Avatar

The Arkadia Saga Complete Series

ABOUT THE AUTHOR

Tiffany Shand is a writing mentor, professionally trained copy editor and copy writer who has been writing stories for as long as she can remember. Born in East Anglia, Tiffany still lives in the area, constantly guarding her workspace from the two cats which she shares her home with.

She began using her pets as a writing inspiration when she was a child, before moving on to write her first novel after successful completion of a creative writing course. Nowadays, Tiffany writes urban fantasy and paranormal romance, as well as nonfiction books for other writers, all available through eBook stores and on her own website.

Tiffany's favourite quote is *'writing is an exploration. You start from nothing and learn as you go'* and it is armed with this that she hopes to be able to help, inspire and mentor many more aspiring authors.

When she has time to unwind, Tiffany enjoys photography, reading, and watching endless box sets. She also loves to get out and visit the vast number of castles and historic houses that England has to offer.

You can contact Tiffany Shand, or just see what she is writing about at:

Author website: tiffanyshand.com

Business site: Write Now Creative

Twitter: @tiffanyshand

Facebook page: Tiffany Shand Author Page

Printed in Poland
by Amazon Fulfillment
Poland Sp. z o.o., Wrocław
11 July 2022

297bab07-4b03-47d0-bbbb-8bee634e297bR01